I0557934

By: Aléce Land

1

Text copyright © 2022 by Jasmine Land

All rights reserved. Published in the United States by Jai Publishing LLC.

ISBN 979-8-9878113-1-3

The Library of Congress has cataloged the softcover edition of this work as follows:

Land, Jasmine.

Humanity's End / by Jasmine Land

Printed in the United States of America

For my parents and grandparents,

Who have always believed in me and encouraged me to pursue my dreams.

Chapter 1:

Potential Trip to Camp

"Two people died yesterday."

That's what my mom tells me while I'm on my way out the door. She said to look at the article she sent, so I click on it when I arrive at the park to meet Olivia. Just as I suspected, it's some weird article talking about the "conspiracy theory."

'James Martin was attacked by an infected female by the name of Susan Wayne in downtown Montgomery, Alabama yesterday afternoon. Wayne bit the victim on his arm and would have done worse if it weren't for law enforcement neutralizing Wayne. The victim was injured and contracted the virus from the woman, so the officers shot Martin as well.'

Oh great. Mom should really stop reading these silly articles. Misinformation like this is responsible for making people believe that there's a *virus* spreading on the East Co-ast. Now some people are in a state of panic. They're too afraid to leave their homes or come into contact with others!

5

As for me, I'm gonna keep doing what I'm doing, because every time an article about this virus comes out, there are no police reports or witnesses to back up these claims! Even the news stations are telling us it's fake! Sadly, my mom believes the fake news, but luckily my stepdad, Hayden, doesn't. At least there's another voice of reason in the house.

"Axel! Snap out of it!" Olivia snaps her fingers at me while we're sitting on lounge chairs at the park house.

"Oh, sorry."

"Is something the matter, Axel?" She raises an eyebrow as if she's dissecting an insect in biology class.

Olivia can also be a "conspiracy theorist" sometimes, so she would probably believe that the virus is real too.

I decide to keep my thoughts to myself. "N-No, nothing's w-wrong." I click on the link that shows the camp I was looking at earlier. "I was just thinking about this camp that I want to go to this summer," I explain.

The website shows kids eating smores, counselors telling spooky stories, and guys playing tug of war.

"Axel Skylark, have I ever told you how bad you are at lying?" Olivia smirks.

"Only a million times. What gives it away?"

"Your voice. You start stuttering a lot," she replies, rolling her eyes in the process.

"I guess I shouldn't be lying in the first place."

"Exactly." She snickers as she takes her pointer finger and pokes my nose.

"But I really do want to go to this camp, and you should too." I emphasize.

Olivia shrugs. "I'm not a big fan of camps or being away from my family," she replies, while nonchalantly flipping through a teen magazine.

"Can't you look at the place, at least? I know how much you like spas, they have one at the camp." I say while raising both eyebrows in hopes that it will pique her curiosity.

Olivia snatches the phone out of my hand and aggressively scrolls through it. She pauses for a moment or two, with a serious look on her face, as if she's an investigator trying to crack a case. Then, she looks at me with excitement in her voice. "Ooh la la! My kind of camp!" She

7

continues scrolling. "Wait—" She lifts her sunglasses up. "It says it's all the way in Georgia!" She dismisses the idea and tosses the phone in my direction.

Luckily, I catch the phone before it hits the ground. "I know it's in Georgia, but it's one of the best camps in America!"

Olivia rolls her eyes. "And how would you know that? One of your weird friends told you?"

I quickly dismiss her comment. "I've been doing some research about popular camps, and this one got a 4.8 rating. I've only been to Georgia a few times, and I liked it, so why not spend one of our last summers of high school there?"

Olivia gets up from her lounge chair. "That's cool and all, but that's way too far from my parents. What if something happens while we're there?"

I lean back in the chair and twirl my dog tag necklace around my finger. "Nothing will happen, but if something did, I'd protect you. I'm practically your older brother anyway."

Olivia folds her arms and looks at me. "YOU protect me? Yeah right! Who are you going to protect me from, a squirrel

8

trying to eat my sandwich?" She bursts out laughing as tears flow from her eyes.

One thing you've gotta learn about Olivia is that she doesn't really have a filter. She tends to say whatever comes to mind without a moment of apprehension.

"Whatever Olivia." I continue scrolling through my phone.

Olivia's my best friend and all, but sometimes she can be annoying.

Oli playfully nudges her shoulder against mine. "I'm just messing with you. I know if you had to, you'd look out for me, but I don't know if I feel comfortable leaving my mom and dad like that."

"So, it's a no?"

"A definite no."

Great. Olivia's completely against going to Georgia, but I've known her for as long as I can remember and one thing she can't resist is a challenge.

I turn my back on Olivia and mumble under my breath. "Well, if you're too afraid to leave your mommy and daddy, I completely understand. You know us "adults" will go to camp and have a good time. I'll make sure to write some letters and let you know how everything goes…Oh, and by the way, does your mommy still leave your night light on for you," I say while trying to cover my mouth from laughing.

She puts her hand on my shoulder and turns me around, so I face her. She gets right in my face (well, as close as she can get to my face she's only five feet).

"Axel. There are no babies here! I'll tell you what, I'll talk to my parents about this. If they say yes… then I MIGHT go." She pauses, tapping her chin. "And by the way, I'll have you know that I stopped sleeping with my night light two years ago!" she says with a condemning expr-ession.

"Good for you, you JUST stopped sleeping with your night light," I chuckle, while positioning my hand for a high-five.

"I said MIGHT- and stop patronizing me!" She replies as she holds up her pointer finger firmly, rejecting my hand.

Me and Olivia are both sixteen years old, and we've been good friends for a while, more specifically, since we were babies. My mom moved to California when I was three and signed me up for daycare in the area. Miss Justine, Olivia's mom, her there and eventually our moms became good friends! Miss Justine always tells me that if it wasn't for her comedic ways, then their friendship would never have existed. My mom, unlike Miss Justine, is an introvert, so it's good to know that she helps Mom *get out of her shell* every now and then. Now I've got a lot of characteristics from my mom, but an introvert is not one of them.

We walk outside of the Parkhouse, and Olivia heads to her bike.

"Alright Axel, see you in a little while." She turns back around. "Why do you want me to go so bad? You can't bear to be away from me?" she teases.

I laugh at her remark. "You wish. All my other friends are busy for the rest of the summer, so you're my last resort," I respond with a smirk.

She rolls her eyes. "*Sure, I am.*" She playfully punches my shoulder. "Oh, by the way, don't forget that my mom and I are coming over to eat smores outside!"

"I won't!" I exclaim, while remembering the stories Olivia told me about her mom and dad cooking smores with her.

I ponder the memories, and kick the dirt with my shoe, letting out a small sigh.

Olivia tilts her head in confusion by the expression on my face. "What's wrong?" She puts her hands on her hips.

"I was just thinking about how cool it would have been to be like you."

She wrinkles her forehead. "What are you talking about?"

I stare at the ground. "I wish I had my dad in my life, like you," I sigh, as I continue to walk toward my car.

Oli pauses for a moment and begins to fight back tears.

She wipes her face and forces a smile. "You still have Hayden! Even if he's just your stepdad, he's a cool guy!"

"Yeah, I guess," I mumble. "I should be grateful."

"Plus!" She looks up at me. "You still have the coolest friend ever!" She shouts with a gleam in her eyes.

I smile.

"No more sadness! We are going to cook these smores outside and enjoy ourselves!" She shouts while punching me in my side.

"Yeah, you're right."

I can always count on Oli for two things; one, to cheer me up and two, to leave a bruise! Man, she can punch hard.

Olivia shakes her head. "How many times do I have to tell you to stop calling me Oli? I hate that nickname."

With a smile on my face, I nod. "Okay, *Oli.*"

Chapter 2:

<u>Coming Home</u>

I pull into the driveway and park my car. "Finally, home." I grab my keys and head inside the house.

"Hey Mom!"

"Hey Axel, how was your day?" she asks as she takes her apron off.

I clearly get my love of cooking and my height from my mom. I often wonder what features or characteristics I have that might be from my dad, but unfortunately, I never met him. I don't really know much about my dad. Usually if I bring him up, my mom gets frustrated and avoids the conversation all together.

All I know for sure is that my dad's name is Reese, and he was in the Air Force Reserves. When my parents got a divorce after three years of marriage, he immediately went into active duty, and my mom soon lost contact with him. He left before my mom knew she was pregnant with me. She tried for years to contact him and tell him about me, but with no success, she eventually gave up.

On a lighter note, she remarried six years ago to a man named Hayden. He's nice and treats us well. I also have a little brother named August. He's four years old.

"My day wasn't bad, I was just trying to convince Olivia to go to that camp I've been talking about all week," I explain as I sit in the dining room chair.

Mom smiles. "Oh? Does she seem interested?" she asks as she ruffles my hair.

"Kinda. She's sort of on the fence, but I think I can pull her to the winning side," I chuckle.

"Well, hopefully she can go."

"Yeah."

She pours me a glass of lemonade and sets a plate of fried fish in front of me.

"Thanks, Mom."

"No problem, sweetie."

August runs in the kitchen with his racecar in his hand. "Mommy! Look at my car! Daddy gave it to me!" He waves the car around.

Mom smiles. "He did? That's pretty cool hun!" She picks August up and kisses his forehead.

"Hey little Aug!" I rub the back of his head.

He giggles. "Hi, Axie!"

I turn my attention back to Mom. "Where's Hayden?" I ask while taking a sip of my lemonade.

Mom yawns. "Working. He's always trying to work overtime, so we can have the best lifestyle possible," she sighs.

Like I previously mentioned, Hayden's a great guy! It's just that sometimes when I mention him, I can't help but think about my own dad.

Mom notices me gazing off in the distance. It's as if she can read my mind.

She smiles at me. "One day you'll meet your dad. Don't worry. I've been consistently praying since the day we lost contact. I want that for you and Reese, and in time, it will happen. Now you go on and finish your dinner."

"Okay." I sit back in the chair and take another bite of my fish.

She clasps her hands together and slides her chair closer to the table. "So, you know how that sickness is going around on the East Coast?" She asks, changing the subject.

I nod my head. "Yeah. You've mentioned it once or twice."

"Well, I'm kind of nervous about you going to the camp in Georgia. People are saying that the virus is really dangerous!" She hesitantly admits.

Mom really needs to stop stressing out about every little thing.

"Mom, you shouldn't believe that nonsense. It's all made up."

Mom has always been over-protective. I appreciate it of course, but sometimes it can be a bit overwhelming.

She sighs, then looks at me with concern. "Sweetie, everyone that has mentioned that sickness is getting silenced. Whether their video is coming down or they can't be interviewed anymore."

"Mom, those people are lying! They're getting shut down because they are giving *false* information!"

17

She turns her head away. "You know what, forget it. We won't agree."

Mom has never been the type to argue. She hates any kind of confrontation, even if it's a much-needed conversation.

"Please don't be mad, Mom…" I sigh.

Mom pauses for a moment before continuing. "So, are you enjoying summer so far?" she asks, disregarding what I said.

"Of course, I am. The mere fact that I don't have to go to school for a few more weeks is awesome."

"That's good."

DRING!

DRING!

The doorbell rings and interrupts our conversation.

"That must be Justine," Mom utters while getting up to open the door.

I follow closely behind her.

She opens the door, and Miss Justine's holding graham crackers in one hand and marshmallows with chocolate in the other.

"Hey Avery and Axe! Look who brought stuff for smores!" Miss Justine shouts as she steps inside the house.

Behind her mother is Olivia, holding a portable stove. "Hey, Axel!" She smiles.

"Hey, Oli!"

I lead them to the backyard and open the screen door. Olivia, Miss Justine, and I sit in lawn chairs on the patio, while Mom fixes the smores, and August runs around the yard with his racecar.

"So, have you been having lots of fun this summer, Axel?" Miss Justine asks.

"Yeah, I guess. I can't complain too much," I respond, while watching Mom toast the marshmallows.

Olivia starts fanning herself with her hand, looking visibly hot. "It is so toasty out here!" she complains. "And my hair isn't making it any better."

Olivia has thick curly hair, so the sun is draining the life out of it...and her.

"Let me help you out, dear." Miss Justine moves closer to Olivia, and starts pulling her hair into a high pony-

19

tail, trying to cool her off and reduce the amount of sweat falling down her neck.

"There you go, hun!"

"Thanks Mom!" Olivia replies while moving a strand of hair that fell in her face.

Miss Justine begins to wind her hair into a bun, in hopes of cooling herself down as well.

Mom walks back to us and sets the smores down on the table. "Dig in!" she exclaims, while grabbing one for herself.

I smile and grab a handful of smores.

"Well, Olivia, did you make your final decision about camp, yet?" I ask, finishing the last bite of a smore.

"I'm not sure, Axe," Olivia shrugs. "I'm on the fence."

"You both should go!" Miss Justine says, while forcing the words out as she chews on a smore.

Mom wipes the residue of a smore off her face and turns her attention to Miss Justine. "Under normal circumstances, I would think it's a great idea, but that outbreak is starting to get out of control on that side of the country. It hasn't traveled to the West Coast yet, and I think it's safer if you guys stayed here."

"Outbreak?" Olivia asks as she tilts her head to the side.

"People believe that it may be a new form of the rabies virus. They aren't sure how it came about, but it's very contagious. If someone encounters an infected person, they could contract it," Mom explains.

Miss Justine shakes her head and starts rubbing my mom's back in hopes of comforting her. "Avery, stop scaring the kids. Look, guys if you want to go... go! You'll be fine. Everyone knows it's a hoax anyway."

Mom slowly looks at Miss Justine and shrugs her shoulders. "Maybe you're right. Maybe I'm just being overprotective. Axel, if you want to go, it's alright with me. I'm sure everything will be fine."

"Yes! Thanks mom!" I put my hand on her shoulder.

"Good for you Axel, but I'm still not sure," Olivia utters.

Mrs. Justine looks over at Olivia. "What are you going to do all summer? Sit on the couch, eat potato chips, and watch reruns of Dreamers…lots of fun," she scoffs, while swirling her finger in the air.

Olivia rolls her eyes and takes a deep breath. "Fine, Axel…I'll go."

I smile and look at Miss Justine. She's just as excited as if she's going too. She gives me a thumbs up. I think she could use a break from Olivia. After all, she is a bit of a complainer.

"How long will it last?" Mom asks.

"The rest of the summer."

Mom sighs deeply. "That's a long time," she frowns, on the verge of changing her mind.

"Mom, we'll be fine. Plus, you two could use the break," I try to convince her.

She sighs once more. "I guess you're right, just, stay safe."

"Well, while they have fun in Georgia, we could go to our cabin up in Michigan, if you'd like?" Miss Justine offers, with her fingers crossed and a child-like smile on her face.

Our moms own this cabin up in Michigan. They originally used it strictly for vacationing. Whenever they needed a break from their kids or husbands, they'd both take a week's trip up there. But now, it's a "storage facility". They store things like food, weapons, and medical supplies in the cabin (which was my mom's idea, because she's so paranoid).

My mom thinks that if anything were to take place in America (power outage, food shortage, virus outbreak), we should have a "safe haven" full of supplies. Miss Justine thought she was just being paranoid but reluctantly agreed anyway. Since then, they haven't really visited it much, because it looks less like a vacation spot and more like an end-of-the-world bunker.

"Yeah, maybe. We haven't been there in so many years, but I guess we could go sometime this summer," Mom smiles.

Olivia wraps her arm around my mom. "I think you guys will have so much fun!"

I nod in agreement. "Me too!"

Chapter 3:

Hayden's Home

"Stop tossing that baseball in the air, Axel." Mom catches the ball in mid-air and puts it in the kitchen drawer.

"When is Hayden going to be here? I still don't get why we have to wait for him to get home before we eat dinner." I stare at my spaghetti in frustration.

"Yeah! I'm hungry now!!!" August shouts while stomping his feet.

"Be patient my little men, he'll be here soon."

As soon as she finishes her sentence, Hayden pushes the front door open and tosses his briefcase on the floor.

"Sorry I took so long. I had a lot of work to finish up at the office." He closes the door and heads to the kitchen sink to wash his hands.

"Hey! Sounds like you had a busy day at work!" Mom sets a bowl of spaghetti down on the table for him.

"Yup. Very busy day!" He sits down and gulps some water down.

"Well, Axel will be leaving in a few days to go to a camp all the way in Georgia," Mom explains.

In shock, Hayden spits all the water out of his mouth right in the direction of August.

August closes his eyes before the rain of saliva and water reach his face.

Mom covers her mouth and bursts into laughter, while Hayden stares at August, processing what just happened.

I grab a napkin and wipe the water off August's face.

"Thank you…" he mumbles.

"Go get cleaned up," Mom chuckles.

I pull August's chair out from under the table, and he takes off running up the stairs and to his room.

I look over at Hayden. "You seem surprised that I'm going all the way to Georgia." I sit back down at the dining table.

Hayden wipes his face with a napkin. "I'm just surprised that Avery would let you go so far away. It's not safe."

25

Mom stays silent for a moment, but her expression screams, *'Hayden is right, you can't go.'*

"But I'm sixteen, I can handle myself. Plus, Mom, you kinda already told Miss Justine that she'd get a break from Olivia."

Mom nods her head. "Yeah, you're right…Justine really does need a break from her," she utters.

Hayden sighs. "Okay, okay. I won't press on the subject any further. It's just that we're all the way in California…It's just so far away."

"Yeah, but like I said, I can handle myself," I reiterate and grab my bowl and place it in the sink.

"He'll be alright, Hayden…" Mom tells him, but I can tell by her voice that she doesn't believe a word she's saying.

"Fine…Just call us if you need anything," Hayden responds while finishing up his dinner.

Chapter 4:

<u>Saying Goodbye</u>

It's been a few days since Mom agreed to let me go to camp. She still feels a little uneasy, but I keep reassuring her. Right now, Olivia completed her packing, so she decided to come over and "oversee" what clothes I'm packing for the trip, since we are leaving tomorrow. As I start putting shirts in my suitcase, I can see in the reflection of the mirror, Olivia replacing the shirts I chose, with shirts that are, "*Olivia approved.*"

I turn around and scold her. "Can you stop? These are the clothes I'm wearing to the summer camp!"

She tosses a shirt on the bed. "Fine, some people don't want to be helped. Even if it's a fashion crisis." She sits down in my beanbag chair. "Man, I hope some of our friends will be at the camp," she announces, changing the subject.

"The chances of that happening are…slim. The camp's a million hours away from home," I shrug, as I pack my last pair of jeans in my suitcase.

"Imagine how bored we might be if we don't know anyone else. This camp will last the rest of the summer," she squirms at the thought of that occurring.

"Look at it this way, Oli, you have an opportunity to meet new people, and they might actually be cool."

I think this will be really good for Oli, because she's always been a bit of a loner. She only has three friends: me, Bella, and…the ugliest, most annoying person on the planet, Selena. *Wow!* Just thought of another great reason to go off to camp…not having to see Selena all summer long.

Olivia slouches a little in the seat. "I guess."

Mom walks into the room and realizes that Olivia looks a little down. "Everything alright?"

"Yeah Miss Avery, everything's fine."

Mom folds her arms, knowing that something is bothering Olivia. "I almost forgot, make sure you two pray. You guys will be far away, and I want to be sure you two will be okay." She bites her nails.

It's a nervous habit she does whenever something is bothering her.

"Ok, Mom. I'll make sure I pray."

Olivia nods in agreement. "Yup. I'll do it Miss Avery."

Mom smiles and walks out of the room.

"Don't worry, Oli, you'll make some friends while we're there," I reassure.

Olivia pauses before responding. "Why do you have so many trophies?" She disregards what I said, and looks at my floating shelf, admiring the awards.

"You're always changing the subject when you feel uncomfortable," I shake my head.

"Not always... But you still didn't answer my question."

"Well, you already know that I've been playing baseball since I was five, and I'm pretty good at it, hence the trophies and medals. You just never go to my games," I shrug, then hop on my bed.

"Well, you know I don't really like sports...Except for track, since I run for our school." She reaches her arms upward, trying to reach one of the trophies.

I grab the trophy off the shelf and hand it to her.

"Thanks, but I didn't need help. I could've grabbed it myself. I'm not that short!"

29

I just stare at her, trying hard not to laugh. "Sure…"

....

I'm right outside the house with Mom and Hayden, getting ready to leave for the airport.

"Are you sure you have everything? Your phone, your clothes, and your—"

"Mom! I have everything, please stop stressing! I'll be fine!" I reach my arms out and hug her tight.

Her eyes begin to get red and puffy, which is an indication that she's about to cry. Hayden notices her expression and begins to rub her shoulder.

"He'll be fine Avery," he reassures, then turns his attention to me. "Make good choices, alright?" He moves his hand from Mom's shoulder to mine.

I smile confidently.

"I always do…most of the time," I chuckle, wheeling my pride back in.

30

August runs outside the house and jumps into my arms. "You better be back, Axie! Or I won't let you play with my car collection anymore!" He yells.

I only play with August's car collection because I enjoy spending time with him.

I ruffle his hair, still holding him in my arms. "Well in that case, I'll be back faster than you can miss me! I promise, August!" I wink as I set him down.

I look back up at Mom, and she's welling up with tears. "I love you so much, honey! You should be on your way, now!" She forces a smile.

I know I'm going to enjoy summer camp, but I know I'm going to miss all of them, too.

BEEP! BEEP!

Olivia honks the horn while waiting in the passenger seat of my car. "Come on, Axel! We're gonna miss our flight if we stay any longer!" She yells out the window.

We all just stare at her. She always wants her way, even if she has to be a little rude to get it.

She notices us looking in disbelief and her face turns red.

"Oh, duh! I'm gonna miss you guys, too!" She waves at them.

Hayden and Mom shake their heads.

"Bye Oli!" August waves at her.

"Bye, August! Please don't call me Oli, though!" she exclaims, while rolling up the window.

I hop in the car and turn to Olivia. "Ready to go, *Oli*?" I tease.

"Just come on!" she laughs.

I put the key in the ignition and back out of the driveway, heading toward the airport.

Chapter 5:

<u>Camp Lovely</u>

Me and Olivia hop out of the car with our suitcases.

"Thanks for dropping us off," I say while throwing my hand up at the taxi driver.

"No problem kids," the man replies while driving away.

"That was the longest flight in history…" Oli drags her feet while pulling her suitcase on the long, unpaved road.

"Do you ever stop complaining? I really think that's just a part of your personality," I joke, putting my arm around her shoulder.

"Do you ever stop being annoying? I think that's a part of YOUR personality!" She quickly pushes my arm off her and walks ahead of me, clearly annoyed by my comment and visibly struggling with her suitcase.

"She's so easily offended," I mumble, catching up to her.

33

I grab her suitcase from her hand and start pulling hers and mine down the road.

She perks up. "Thanks, Axe!" She smiles as she continues to walk ahead.

I nod.

Olivia's phone makes a weird jingle noise. "Oh! My mom texted me!" She immediately reads the text.

I look over her shoulder and read it as well.

'Have fun at camp! I know I'll have fun on my vacation without ya!' with a bunch of winky face emojis after it.

Olivia stares at the phone for a second. "Is it just me, or does my mom seem a little too happy about me leaving for a few weeks?"

"Are you kidding? She's gonna miss you like crazy!" I tell her while holding my laughs inside.

Oli briskly walks ahead of me. "You're right, who wouldn't miss me?" She smirks.

I look around the entrance of the Summer Camp. It looks nothing like the one online. It looks old and rugged. There was supposed to be a large sign that read, 'Welcome to Camp Loving!' But all I see is an old sign that says, 'Welcome to Camp Lovely!' I think Mom might have signed me and Oli up for the wrong camp, but in the right state…

Olivia raises her sunglasses as she stares at the entrance. "This is not what it looked like online!" Her face slowly turns red.

I let out a nervous chuckle. "Yeah, I think my mom accidentally signed us up for the wrong camp. Now we'll be spending the rest of our summer here…at some old summer camp."

She rolls her eyes. "This is why I should have made the arrangements. I would have signed us up for the right camp, but I guess we have to live with this," she groans.

"OLIVE!!" A familiar voice yells.

I know that annoying voice anywhere. It can't be…*please no…*

I look to my left and see a thin girl with long black hair and pale skin.

WHY! Why did she have to be here?

I start squirming as I see her approaching us, her heels clicking on the road.

"SELENA!!!" Olivia yells back. They run up to each other as if they haven't seen one another in years, but they just saw each other a few days ago!

I shake my head from side to side. I thought I could escape her for the summer. Here's a little history lesson on the evil witch that lives a neighborhood over.

Selena is so annoying. She's not that bright, but she somehow makes everyone (except me) think she is. Olivia met Selena in the third grade, and when Selena found out that Oli had another best friend, me, she felt like we had to compete for Olivia's attention. Ever since that day, she's always tried to make me look bad in front of Olivia, which she's doing a terrible job at.

Anytime she sees me, she wrinkles her little nose and frowns. She's bad enough at home but having her here at camp, ruining my trip, is really going to make me mad!

"It's good to see you!" Selena exclaims while hugging her.

Olivia grins. "Yeah! I didn't think you'd actually come all this way to camp with me!"

"Well, I couldn't let you come here without your bestie!" She snickers, while flipping her long black hair out of her face.

Wow. So, you mean to tell me that Olivia told her to come? She knows I can't stand her. She could've at least warned me!

"But why did you want to come here anyway?" Selena raises her pointy eyebrow.

"Axel begged me to."

I shake my head. If it was anyone else, I would have explained that Olivia was stretching the truth, but at this point, I could care less about what Selena thinks.

"Of course, he wanted you to come, he has no other friends. Who's he gonna ask?" She laughs sinisterly, but it seems like Olivia doesn't notice.

Me and Selena's eyes meet, and she instantly wrinkles her nose and frowns her face (she can't help doing that anytime she sees me).

"Why did Axel want to come to such an old ugly camp anyway? Did he want something to match his appearance?" She cackles with laughter.

As I'm about to respond, Olivia puts her hand on my shoulder and signals not to say anything. I look at her for a moment before taking a deep breath and biting my tongue.

Olivia sighs in relief and turns to Selena. "Well, his mom signed us up for the wrong camp. I wish I knew that before I sent you the name of this place."

Selena pouts. "Yeah, I wish you did, too. When I was signing up for the camp, I was really confused by the photos of this place, but I didn't question it...I should've." She makes eye contact with me once again.

Olivia wrinkles her eyebrows in Selena's direction. I think we both know that Selena's about to say more unpleasant things about me.

"Axel? You had to drag Olive out here to camp, because you can't play in the play pin like a big boy by yourself?" she asks in a baby voice and bursts into laughter.

Olivia covers her mouth and giggles softly.

Really, Oli?

"What's the matter Selena? There's no Godzilla convention this summer, so you had to find something else to occupy your time?" I smirk.

Selena grunts and rolls her eyes.

"Yeah, keep rolling your eyes Selena. Maybe you'll find a brain back there."

Olivia stands between me and Selena. "That's enough, Axel."

My eyes widen. "Why are you looking at me? She's the one who started it!"

Olivia, not wanting to be in the middle of an argument between her two closest friends, does what any reasonable person would do, she changes the subject.

Olivia looks down at the ground and notices Selena's shoes. "Oh my goodness, Selena! Are those new heels? I've got to get me a pair!" She giggles as they walk further into the campground.

I reluctantly follow behind them and try to tune out Selena's annoying voice. We follow the road until we reach a platform that a tall man with a large belly and overalls is standing on. He starts rubbing his stomach as if he's carrying an eight-pound baby.

"Good morning kiddos! My name is Counselor James and welcome to Camp Lovely, where we want you to

39

love one another and love this camp! Before we reach our actual camping grounds, choose a group of three to pair with."

It's hard to keep my focus on what he is saying, because he clearly just got through eating a glazed donut and the residue is all over his face.

As I'm trying to pay attention, I notice Olivia reuniting with her other best friend, Bella. *Did Olivia send out a text for all of them to meet here?*

Bella waves hello, and I wave back.

Bella is the nicest of the group—in my opinion—and the quietest (don't get me wrong, Oli is nice sometimes but Bella's nicer). My problem with her is that she's Selena's minion. She listens to everything she says, apart from being mean to me (most of the time). I just don't get why Olivia didn't warn me that they were coming.

Olivia swings her head around and looks at me. "You don't mind being in a separate group from me, right?"

"Obviously not, why would I?" I shrug.

Olivia looks reassured, and she continues talking to her friends.

Now I just need to find someone to group with. Shouldn't be a problem.

I look to my right and see a guy about 6 feet tall with short, brown hair.

I head over to him, feeling a little short next to him, even though I'm around 5'10, so he's not that much taller than me, but still.

"Hey, want to be in a group?" I ask.

He turns to the side and nods in agreement. "I'd prefer to be by myself, but since this is mandatory...sure," he replies nonchalantly in a cocky tone.

I extend my hand. "Well, I'm Axel Skylark."

He chuckles. "Why so formal? Most people tend to wave or nod to say hello, but you're getting ready to shake my hand?" He can't help but burst into laughter.

I didn't find anything amusing. However, I chuckle to lighten the mood.

He starts wiping the tears that fell from the corner of his eyes while he was laughing. "My name is Weston, and I don't really do handshakes." He folds his arms as he waits for the counselor to finish talking.

41

Counselor James claps his hands three times to get our attention. "Now that the chatter is to a minimum, does everyone have a group of three?"

I raise my hand. "We don't."

Weston looks at me. "Bro, why did you say anything? We would have been fine." He puts his hand on his forehead and mumbles, "I'm already regretting coming here."

I shake my head. "Look, he asked a question, and all I did was answer it."

"Tsk."

That's all he said. I want to ask him what his problem is but judging by the muscles protruding from his long sleeve shirt, that probably won't be a good idea. I'm not saying I'm weak or anything, because trust me, I'm not. But I know there are some battles that just aren't worth fighting.

"Well, is there anyone that's not in a group?" Counselor James asks impatiently while tapping his foot on the ground.

A girl raises her hand. She looks no older than ten.

"You've gotta be kidding me. Anyone but Marianne." He puts his hand over his face.

"Oh, so you know her?" I question.

He just rolls his eyes. "I don't think we're going to get along very well," he mumbles. "Since you're so curious, yes, I do know her. I didn't think I'd know anyone here," he explains, while grabbing his water bottle.

"What's the deal with her?" I inquire.

"You are an extremely inquisitive kid," Weston chuckles, while shaking his head.

"Kid? What are you, a year older than me?" I roll my eyes.

Weston shrugs. "Well, depends on how old you are."

"I'm sixteen."

"Well, I'm seventeen, so I guess you were right. But anyway," he takes a sip of his water before continuing. "Back to the little girl, her name's Marianne, and she's my sister's friend. She's kind of annoying. She talks a lot, kind of like you!" He laughs.

I completely ignore him. I honestly don't have time for negative people. I already deal with Olivia and her attitude problem, and I don't want to deal with anyone else's.

Counselor James points to me and Weston. "Well sweetheart, you can join those boys right over there."

She skips along the path and stops when she sees Weston. "Hi Weston, who's your friend?" she asks in a high-pitched voice.

She has long, brown hair pulled up in a ponytail. She also has big hazel eyes, and she's wearing a pink shirt with jeans.

"He's not my friend, I just met him! His name's Axel though."

"Well, hello Weston's non-friend Axel," she giggles.

"Hi Marianne. It's nice to meet you," I respond.

Marianne smiles. "Oh, I see Weston's already told you my name." She turns to Weston. "How is Willow doing? I haven't seen her in a few days."

Weston nods. "She's good." He gazes off in the distance. "The only good thing about my mom forcing me to go to camp is that I can get away from Willow. No more teatime, no more turning the rope while she jumps, and most of all, no more babysitting…At least till the end of summer. I can also get a break from my other responsibilities…" he mumbles to himself.

I disregard what he says. Clearly if he wanted to talk more about it, he wouldn't have mumbled.

"Now that everyone has their group and are ready to go, place your cellular devices in this bin. No technology for the rest of the summer unless authorized by a counselor," Counselor James explains.

I smack my hand on my forehead. "Great. This camp is getting better and better."

Weston shakes his head. "Tell me about it."

All of us put our phones in the bin...except Selena.

"No! I cannot live without my phone! I need it to survive!" She screams, holding her phone tightly.

"So, all I've needed to do all these years was take your phone and you'd be a distant memory?" I smirk.

"Shut up, Axel!" She shouts.

"Anyway," Olivia rolls her eyes. "Selena, it's not that big of a deal. If something important is going on, I'm sure the counselors will tell us."

"Ugh, fine..." Selena hesitantly tosses her phone in the bin and holds back tears.

Counselor James hands the bin to another counselor. "Alright, now that we have the phones, follow me."

As we all follow the counselor, it doesn't take long for Marianne to start rambling off questions.

"How old are you?" Marianne tilts her head to the side.

"I'm sixteen," I tell her, as I glance over at Olivia and her group.

"I'm eight and a half," She responds while looking in the same direction as me. "Do you know them? Are they your friends?"

I raise my eyebrow. "Yes, I know them, but I'm only friends with one of them."

"Which one?" She asks.

Not to agree with Weston or anything, but I kinda know what he meant when he said she talks a lot.

"The one with the long wavy hair," I walk ahead, hoping that she gets the idea that I don't really feel like talking.

She walks faster, so she's at the same pace as me. "Did you want to group with them?"

46

Weston chuckles to himself and shakes his head, happy that she has someone else to nag.

"Of course I want my friend in my group, it's just that I'm not in the mood for them talking about makeup and hair products."

"Well, I can call them over here!"

"That won't be necessary, Marianne," Weston interjects with a frustrated voice. "Can't you see that you're bothering him? You're so annoying."

Marianne, not being phased at all by his comment, skips the rest of the way to the camping grounds.

I get the feeling that he doesn't like her much. I mean yeah, she does talk a lot, but he didn't have to be rude to her. We turn a corner and arrive at the actual campgrounds.

Chapter 6:

<u>The Campgrounds</u>

The campgrounds look like an old camp from the '70s. The trees are bending which is causing them to touch the roofs of the five small cabins in the near distance, the wood from the cabins are starting to change color from being weathered on for so many years, and there's a mess hall that, from the outside, looks like no place I'd want to eat at!

I really wish Hayden (or ANYONE else) signed me and Olivia up for camp, because we wouldn't have been at this dump.

Counselor James waves his hand in the air to get our attention. "I haven't introduced the counselor for the girls yet. As you all probably figured out, I'm the head counselor for the boys, and Jennifer is the head counselor for the girls."

Jennifer raises her hand.

Counselor James scratches his arm and lets out a loud yawn. "Alright! Boys say bye to the girls. We're going our separate ways till campfire time in a few minutes."

I scratch my chin in confusion. "So, what was the point of having a group, and why are we having 'campfire time' during the day?"

Marianne picks a dandelion from off the ground and blows on it. "I have no idea, but I'll see you during supper!" She skips over to Olivia and her friends.

Weston rubs the sweat off his forehead. "I told you she talks a lot."

"Yeah, she does, but she kind of grows on you," I reply while following behind the counselor.

Weston shakes his head and mumbles something under his breath, but I can't quite hear what he said. *I just know he probably mumbled something rude.*

Counselor James stops in front of two cabins in the wilderness. "These are the two cabins y'all boys have. There are two bunks in one cabin and three in the other cabin. Good thing there are only ten of you."

"What's the other cabin over there?" A guy points to a cabin further away.

"Oh, that's just the counselor cabin. Choose your bunkmates while I use the counselor bathroom," he explains as he walks away.

I shake my head. Counselor James doesn't strike me as the kind of guy that would wash his hands once he's done.

"Hm. Guess I'll have to choose some bunkmates." I observe a group of guys a few feet from me.

One of the guys stomps his foot on the ground. "Ugh! I hate this stupid camp!"

"I know right! This place is trash!" another adds.

Well, I'm not bunking with them.

I notice Weston making his way toward the "complainers" and it seems like he's going to bunk with them, and I have NO problem with that. He's not good company anyway.

Out of nowhere, I hear an ear-piercing whistle blow. I quickly cover my ears to prevent my ear drums from bursting! I look around and see Counselor James holding his whistle in his hand.

He wipes his nose on his sleeve and slides the whistle in his back pocket. "Alright it seems like everyone has made their choice of bunkmates!"

I turn and notice a few guys standing near me, so I guess I'll be bunking with them.

"You boys head to the cabins, while I bring another male counselor out here." Counselor James marches to the counselor cabin.

Me and my group walk silently to the larger cabin with three bunk beds.

"Ever hear about the scary TRUE stories about this place?" One of the guys ask.

I guess the guy figures it's a good way to break the ice.

I chuckle. Don't get me wrong, some stories are true, but there are always terrifying stories about every camp, and they usually end up being fake.

"I don't know why you're laughing, but these are facts! Jeremy never lies," another boy says.

The two boys are identical twins. They both are average height with brown hair. The one that's talking about

51

the scary stories, Jeremy, has big, black-framed glasses. The other one has a mouth full of braces.

"Look, Jeremy, is it? I don't believe in that kind of thing anymore. I've been tricked too many times." I continue down the path.

Jeremy rubs his chin. "Eh. People never believe in that stuff until they see it for themselves. By the way, what's your name?"

"I'm Axel."

"And I'm Jeffrey, his twin brother." As he smiles, his braces shimmer in the sunlight. He holds the cabin door open as we step inside.

The other three kids stay silent and just hop on their bunks. One of the kids has his nose in a comic book, turning the pages eagerly.

I look around the cabin and notice the lack of cleanliness. It's not terrible...It's just that the furniture is old and covered in dust. There's also a lot of crumbs on the ground, so they probably haven't cleaned this place in a long time.

"This cabin could have been a lot cleaner," I announce while wiping my hands on a bunk and seeing the amount of dust that rubs off.

"That's a lot of dust! I wonder when's the last time they dusted around here!" Jeremy exclaims, easing closer to the bunk.

"They probably haven't dusted since the 1920s," I jokingly reply.

Jeremy wrinkles his forehead. "Actually, if they haven't dusted since the 1920s, there would be a lot more dust in this cabin," he corrects.

I let out a deep sigh. "It was a joke."

Jeffrey rubs the back of his head in embarrassment. "Sorry about my brother, he's basically interested in a lot of things and likes getting everything 'scientifically accurate'. He's definitely the smarter twin," he states while placing his arm around Jeremy.

"I am inclined to agree with you. I take my studies very seriously. However, Jeffrey here is successful in the arena of sports and popularity. He is the quarterback for our high school football team," Jeremy replies.

"Well, football's never been my strong suit, but I've played baseball for as long as I can remember," I explain.

"Nice! I've always enjoyed watching baseball, I've just never been good at it," Jeremy replies.

The speakers turn on and a male voice says, "Everyone please gather to the campfire for camp stories and smores!"

I nod my head. "Yes! I never get tired of smores." I open the cabin door.

"Me neither!" Jeremy announces while taking off toward the campfire.

"Wait up!" Jeffrey yells while following behind his brother.

I walk out of the cabin and notice Weston standing outside. "Hey Weston, enjoying your group?" I ask him.

Weston folds his arms. "They're alright. They just complain too much," he admits, "and that's saying a lot coming from me. What about yours?"

"They're cool."

Weston nods and we both head toward the campfire.

Chapter 7:

Scary Stories and Smores

We finally arrive at the campfire, and the girls are already gathered around it. There are a few log benches surrounding the firepit, so I look around in hopes of seeing Olivia nearby. As I scan the vicinity, I notice Olivia waving at me, signaling me to sit next to her, but so is Marianne.

"Guess you've gotta choose which one to sit next to," Weston chuckles while pointing at both.

Marianne seems nice and all, but Olivia is my best friend, so I guess I'll sit beside her.

As I take a seat beside Olivia and her friends, I see Marianne's smile quickly turn into a frown. I let out a sigh and look at Olivia.

"Hey Oli."

Before Olivia can respond, Selena bursts into laughter.

"Oli? He still calls you that trashy name?"

Olivia frowns. "Sadly…"

Bella stares at the ground below her. "Y-Yeah, it is kinda trashy," she mimics, while refraining from making eye contact with me.

Why can't she have her own opinion?

Olivia takes a bite of her smore. "The nickname isn't *trashy*," she snaps. "I just don't like it," she reveals while elbowing me.

Marianne observes the insult from a distance and makes her way over to me, Olivia, Bella, and Selena. "What's so funny?" she asks.

Selena wrinkles her forehead and turns to Olivia, then back at Marianne. "Little girl, how 'bout you mind your business."

I interrupt. "There's no reason to be rude Selena, like you said, she's just a little kid."

Marianne wrinkles her eyebrows and stomps her foot. "I'm not a little kid! I'm eight and a half!"

"You are a little girl to us!" Selena affirms.

Marianne stares at Selena with her beaty little eyes. She notices that Selena is much older than her, and that she wouldn't be able to win the dispute, so she storms off and slouches in a seat next to Weston.

"Can you stop being so rude, Selena? You take pleasure in making others miserable, and it's so annoying," I respond, defending Marianne.

Selena gives me the death stare. "No one was talking to you Axel!"

"I don't need an invitation to join the conversation—"

"Why don't you introduce me to your friend, Axel? Seems like you wasted no time finding new ones," Oli abruptly interrupts, mumbling the last part.

I look at Olivia. "I don't know why you're irritated, but I don't know if I'd consider her my friend since she's so much younger than me. Her name is Marianne, though."

"Oh Axel, it's okay if she's your friend! We get that you can't make any friends your age!" Selena laughs hysterically.

"You are so childish Selena. Frankly, it's disgusting," I snap.

Olivia puts her hand on Selena's shoulder. "He's right, that was a little childish."

Selena folds her arms and pouts.

Counselor James overhears us talking and claps his hands. "I will not tolerate y'all being rude to one another! We just want you all to have fun! Now, let's just start our camp stories."

Olivia frowns at me and whispers, "I thought you would act more mature than this."

I look at her with a confused expression on my face and immediately reply. "What are you talking about? Your friend was the one acting like a five-year-old."

"Whatever, Axel."

Selena gives me a scolding glare. "COUNSELOR! THIS KID KEEPS TALKING DURING THE STORY!" She points her crooked finger at me.

Counselor James points to a seat across the fire pit. "Sit there, maybe it will stop your mouth from running during the story."

I stand up. "But she was the one that—"

"Nope, nope, nope. I don't wanna hear any nonsense. Just please go over there," he orders.

I frown and walk over to where the counselor points, which coincidently is right beside Weston. I sit on the log beside him, and he shakes his head in disbelief.

"Your friend seems like a jerk," he whispers to me.

There's a shock. Most people think that with Olivia's big bright smile and leadership skills, she would never say an unkind word, but that's far from the truth. Don't get me wrong, Olivia *can* be nice, but that's not typically her first emotion. Either way, he's not wrong, she is acting like a jerk, but I would never admit that to him.

"She's not a jerk."

"Come on Axel, we both know she is."

"Look, it doesn't matter whether I think that or not, she's my best friend, and I'd rather not talk about her behind her back."

I may not always agree with what Olivia says or does all the time, but she's my best friend, and I'm loyal to her.

"Whatever, but if she really is your best friend, she should treat you better."

I ponder on his words while I listen to the camp story.

"There once was a counselor that watched over cabin number nine." Counselor James walks around each camp goer slowly. "Some days he occasionally took naps in the cabin before the day was over, because he was so tired," he remarks while raising one eyebrow and shining the flashlight in his face. "One sizzling summer day, everyone was at the lake trying to catch fish. As they were fishing, the counselor grew tired and decided to stay in cabin number nine for the rest of the day."

Marianne's teeth start chattering during the story. "This is so scary…" she whispers under her breath.

Counselor James stands in front us with a creepy smile upon his face, his voice turns to a whisper. "While the counselor was napping, a man that was undead slowly crept up on the counselor and took a chunk out of him!" Counselor James jumps toward us and yells, "The counselor became undead instantly!" He points in the direction of the cabins. "Some say they can still hear the undead counselor in cabin number nine snoring, like nothing ever happened…"

"I love these spooky tales!" Jeremy announces while clasping his hands together. Him and Jeffrey are sitting two logs over and yet, I can still hear Jeremy as clearly as if he was right beside me.

60

Chapter 8:

<u>Back in the Cabin</u>

The cabin is pretty small. There's barely enough space for any of us to walk around since there are three bunkbeds in here and a small desk with a chair underneath, but that's the least of my worries. The hinges on the bathroom door are rusted (it'll probably break any minute now), and some pieces of the hardwood floor are loose.

I step in the bathroom and change into a red T-shirt and black joggers.

KNOCK! KNOCK!

"Hurry up, Axel! Nature calls!" Jeremy yells while banging on the bathroom door.

"Okay, okay! I'm coming!" I open the bathroom door, and Jeremy pushes me out of the way and slams the door shut.

"Hey! The hinges are messed up as is! Don't make them any worse!" Jeffrey shouts from the other end of the cabin.

I walk over to my bunkbed and my bunkmate is waiting for me to make the choice. *The top or the bottom bunk.*

"I choose the bottom," I tell Rob, my bunkmate, while tossing my bag on the old bed.

"You sure you don't want the top one?" Rob asks.

"Nah, I prefer to be on the bottom one, just in case I need to make a run for it," I chuckle, pretending to run.

Rob starts laughing. "Yeah, but I think I'll be the safest, because there could be an alien invasion and they grab the first kid they see!" he explains while hiding behind the bed.

Me and Jeffrey stare at Rob.

"How old are you?" Jeffrey asks as he scratches his head.

Rob smiles. "I'm 14!"

Jeffrey and I continue staring at him. He looks around that age, but based on his comment, I thought he was younger.

Rob hops on the top bunk. "Well, I'm going to get some sleep!"

Jeffrey nods his head. "Yeah, I guess it's time we all get some sleep. The other two boys are already fast asleep on their beds."

As Jeffrey finishes, Jeremy pushes the bathroom door open. "This bathroom is really old…We might as well have port-a-potties." He closes the bathroom door behind him.

I laugh at his comment and lay on my bed. The first day of camp wasn't the best, but I suppose it can only go up from here.

....

As morning arrives, I wake up to the sound of ear-piercing whistles blowing.

"Why are the whistles so loud…" I mumble, rubbing my eyes.

"I have no idea," Jeffrey murmurs.

I open my eyes and notice that Jeremy and Jeffrey are wearing matching outfits. They have blue jeans on with a black short-sleeved shirt.

63

"You guys are gonna be really hot with those black shirts," I tell them as I grab my clothes from my suitcase.

"That's true, since black absorbs heat more than other colors." Jeremy rubs his chin.

"Yeah! The sun has some crazy absorbing powers, so only some things are affected by it!" Rob interrupts.

"So anyway," Jeffrey places his hand on his forehead. "I personally like the heat, Jeremy on the other hand just wanted to match my outfit like we're ten years old or something." He mumbles the last few words, not wanting to hurt his brother's feelings.

I open the bathroom door and quickly change into my outfit. Once I change, I stick my nametag on my shirt and follow my bunkmates out of the cabin.

"It took you boys long enough!" Counselor James frowns his face.

I stare at him with confusion. "I mean, we had to get dressed first—"

Counselor James leans in close to see my nametag. "When the whistle blows, you come outside instantly! No questions asked *Axel*."

64

I roll my eyes. I really wish Mom signed me up for the right camp.

"Now, let's head to the cafeteria for some breakfast." Counselor James leads the way toward the mess hall.

....

"Just grab a tray and grab the food you want," Counselor James explains as he makes his way over to the other counselors.

The cafeteria looks really old. There are cracks throughout the ceiling, so I know this place has been around for a long time. There's also a gross stench coming from the kitchen, and the lights keep flickering on and off. *I'm not so sure I want to eat breakfast again...*

"Man, if I knew this place looked like this, I would've just stayed in a one-star hotel," Weston jokes as he walks in line ahead of me.

I nod my head. "Tell me about it."

"This food looks disgusting!" Olivia shouts as she slams the tray on the counter.

65

"I don't care little girl, just eat. You need nutrition," a cook grunts as she wipes her nose with her hand and rubs it on her apron.

"Unbelievable!" Olivia pushes the tray and storms out of the cafeteria.

"I think I'll pass as well. There are at least 40 different germs all over those utensils you are using." Jeremy pushes his tray to the side and sits down at one of the long, wooden tables.

"That goes for me too," Jeffrey mumbles as he makes his way over to the table Jeremy's sitting at.

"Yeah, same." Weston follows behind Jeffrey.

I glance at the food and back at the kitchen staff.

I'm really hungry, but those people in the kitchen are disgusting. I can't trust them to fix my food.

I push the cafeteria doors open and make my way outside. As I close the doors behind me, I notice Olivia sitting on the grass and eating a bag of beef jerky nearby.

I sit on the grass beside her. "You have food?"

She stares at me and shoves the bag behind her.

"I already saw the bag of beef jerky, Olivia."

Oli, with a guilty look on her face, pulls the bag from behind her. "I wanted to bring a bunch of beef jerky sticks on our camping trip, just in case I didn't like the food. Thank goodness I thought of it." She finishes the last bite of a jerky stick.

"Wow! So, you snuck out of the cafeteria to eat beef jerky and didn't even tell me about it. I bet you didn't even bring any for me."

She reaches her hand in her bag and hands me a stick of jerky. "Of course I did! I would never leave you out!"

"Right...But thanks." I chow down on the jerky, and my stomach starts to settle.

"That's what friends are for, I guess..." she mumbles as she takes another bite of jerky.

The counselor's whistle goes off again, and we continue our activities.

....

67

"Alright! Our final activity will be tug of war! The winner of this game will get to use their phone for TEN minutes!" Counselor James tells us.

"Ooh! I need to see what I've been missing out on!" Selena squeals.

"TEN MINUTES?! That's barely enough time to do anything!" Weston grunts.

Counselor James leans close to Weston. "It's either that, or no tech at all."

Weston mumbles something under his breath and steps back.

"Your team will be whoever is in YOUR CABIN. You will compete AGAINST YOUR OWN GENDER and see who wins. There will be a winning team for the boys, and a winning team for the girls," he explains.

I'm paired with Rob, Jeremy, Jeffrey, and the two boys that I've barely spoken to, since we're all bunkmates. I would've preferred having Weston on my team, because he's got a lot more muscle than all these guys combined.

"Ready, set... BATTLE!" Counselor James blows his whistle, and the game begins.

I grind my shoes in the dirt and start pulling as hard as I can. As I pull with all my might, we start moving forward...straight into the ground. My face meets the dirt, and it isn't a great first impression! Weston's team won with no problems.

"Need a hand?" Weston helps me up.

"Thanks. Your team won by a landslide," I chuckle.

"Yeah, I guess that means I get to use my phone for a few minutes."

Out of nowhere, a guy on my team (one that I've barely spoken to) walks up and pushes me to the ground. I hit the ground hard on my back, and my green baseball cap flies off my head.

"You're such a loser! We lost because of you!" he shouts.

For the record, me and this guy are the reason why our team didn't fall to the ground instantly, so I don't know why he's mad at me!

In a flash, I get up and brush the dirt off my pants. "Hey! You better not do that again!" I yell.

As the boy steps closer to me, I realize how tall he is. *He's probably 6'3.* I glance around and notice a crowd forming around us.

Well, I definitely can't back down now.

"What'd you say?" The guy asks while pounding his fist in his hand.

As my eyes meet with Olivia's, she lowers her head and covers her face with her hands, like she can't bear to watch what's gonna happen next. I'm not gonna lie, I'm not a fighter, because I've never had to fight anyone. But when it comes down to it, I know I can still defend myself if I have to.

I take a deep breath, and my voice cracks a little. "I said…"

At that moment, Weston steps forward. He stands beside me and cracks his knuckles.

"Hey, Mike? He's with me."

Immediately, I step back, and Weston is standing face to face with the guy, Mike. All of a sudden, Mike's angry face turns into a smile, and he puts his fists down.

"Oh Weston! If I knew he was with you, I would've left him alone."

Weston in turn, pats the guy on the chest. "Yeah Mike, I know. Just don't let it happen again." And with that, he heads to his cabin.

"Sure thing, Wes. No problem." The guy reaches down and picks up my cap, knocks the dust off of it, and hands it back to me. "Here you go."

I reluctantly take my hat back and follow Weston.

"Hey, thanks for that," I tell him.

"No problem," Weston says nonchalantly.

"But you know, I could've handled it."

"Yeah, I'm sure you could've, but isn't better to avoid conflict?" he asks.

Hm. I thought Weston was just a self-centered guy, but maybe I judged him a little too harshly.

I continue following him down the path. "Yeah, you're right. Thanks again, I appreciate it."

"Yup."

Curiosity is getting the best of me.

"So, you know that kid?" I probe.

"Yeah."

"Well?"

Weston groans. "We go to the same high school."

"Well, you made Mike back down so quick, so you must have quite the reputation."

I hear footsteps coming from behind me, and I look to see who it is. *Oh, it's just Jeffrey, Jeremy, and Rob.*

Jeffrey clears his throat. "Weston, right?"

Weston nods his head as he continues walking.

"Well, that was pretty cool what you did back there, looking out for Axel and all," Jeffrey grins.

Rob laughs. "That poor kid was stuttering so much, he could barely respond to you!"

Weston chuckles. "Yeah, he knows better than to mess with me."

"I must admit Weston, I was nervous after you stepped in. Afterall, it was clear that he was looking for a fight," Jeremy responds.

"Yeah, Mike might've been looking for one, but he knew he didn't want one with me," Weston replies while kicking his cabin door open.

Chapter 9:

<u>Just Like the Movies</u>

As I'm fast asleep, I suddenly hear a loud scream! My eyes widen as I quickly hop out of my bed. "What's wrong?!"

Jeremy and Jeffrey turn around.

"Sorry, that was Jeremy. He's just a little freaked out."

Jeremy sits at the foot of my bed. "A little? More like a lot! Remember the story that Counselor James told us the night before, about the Undead Tale...?"

"Yeah, what about it?"

"Well, we keep hearing strange noises outside, and our counselor hasn't checked on us in a while."

All the noise wakes Rob up too. He jumps off the top bunk with excitement as if he's been waiting all his life for a moment like this.

"You seriously think it's the Undead Tale?" I tilt my head to the side, looking at Jeremy in disbelief.

"YES! I'm not crazy!"

"He's right man. We are in cabin number nine," Jeffrey replies.

I shrug. "Let's just ask what the other kids think." I shake Mike on the bottom bunk (next to mine), and he wakes right up. "Hey again—"

"What do you want? It's not like Weston's in here to defend you." He cuts his eyes.

"First of all," I clear my throat, "I didn't need Weston to defend me. He just did because we're friends, I guess." I lean closer to Mike. "Second of all, keep bothering me, and you're gonna wish Weston was here to stop me from beating you down." I give him a look like, 'bro, I am not joking'.

I stand there, forcing myself to stare at him and not look away. Hopefully he'll believe what I said, because like I mentioned before, I'm no fighter.

Mike shakes his head, knowing that a fight with me now means a fight with Weston later. "Fine, whatever. Just leave me alone." He turns away from me and lays back down.

I smile with satisfaction.

"That was so cool, Axel!" Rob gives me two thumbs up and Jeremy and Jeffrey nod in unison.

I smile at them and shake the other guy on the top bunk.

"Um, sorry to bother you, but—" I immediately stop talking and am caught off guard by how he looks.

The guy's eyes are a grayish white. His skin is no longer a tannish complexion like before, now it's really pale. He suddenly starts groaning and out of nowhere, he leaps off the bed and tries to bite me!

With all my might, I hold him up as his teeth try to sink into my skin. "AHHH! GET HIM OFF ME!"

Jeremy grabs a broom and pushes the kid into the bathroom. As he does so, Jeffrey quickly shuts the door and Rob helps me up.

"Are you ok!?" they ask.

"Yeah..." I say while shivering. Goosebumps are up and down my arms.

"Hopefully that bathroom door will hold him!" Rob yells.

Mike hops out of his bed in shock. "What just happened?!"

"Axel was attacked by your bunkmate! He started groaning and his skin turned all pale! It was so weird!" Jeffrey explains.

"Why didn't you just beat him up, Axel?" Mike asks while chuckling to himself.

I wipe the sweat away from my brow and look at Mike.

"This is no laughing matter. Something is seriously wrong!" I reply, in hopes of drawing attention away from the topic.

Jeremy interrupts. "Axel, *now* do you think it could be the Undead Tale?"

I start to remember what Mom said about that virus going around the East Coast, but I didn't take it seriously before...Now I'm starting to believe that it may be true.

"That's a possibility," I mumble and scratch my head. "But maybe it's the virus that people were talking about."

Jeremy and Jeffrey start laughing.

77

"That virus is not real! There is no tangible evidence that any of those "cases" ever occurred!" Jeremy cackles.

"Oh, but the Undead Tale is real?" I rebuttal.

Jeremy and Jeffrey are no longer laughing. Instead, they appear to be deep in thought.

I think about what I said to my mom and Hayden. I told them that there was nothing to worry about and that the virus wasn't real.

I'm starting to second guess that.

Rob shrugs his shoulders. "I believe that the virus could be real. It's not too farfetched," Rob agrees while shrugging his shoulders.

Honestly, I think that's the first sentence Rob has said that didn't include something about a comic book or a video game.

"Hm." Jeffrey rubs his hand on his chin. "I guess anything is possible."

"There's no way that virus is real. That guy is probably just tired or something," Mike shrugs.

"I've heard someone's eyes turning red when they're tired, but never a grayish white!" Jeremy responds.

78

I stand up. "Well, whatever it is, we should go find Counselor James and tell him what happened."

Jeremy, Jeffrey, and Rob nod in agreement.

Mike looks at all of us with a blank stare. Although he knows what I'm saying is possible, he'll do anything to keep from agreeing with me...Even if it means sacrificing everyone's safety.

I don't know why this guy hates me so much.

Mike lays back on the bed with his arms behind his head and his feet crossed. "I have better things to do, like, live in reality and not in this fantasy world of yours. I'll be getting some rest while you guys follow Axel out in the woods...in the middle of the night. You guys have fun with that!"

"Well, Good luck! We all know that bathroom door is bound to break at any moment, so just be aware," Jeremy responds.

Mike raises his hand and shoos us out the door.

79

Chapter 10:

<u>Looking for Everyone</u>

I ease out of the front door with my bunkmates close behind. I'm not sure if it's in my imagination or not, but tonight seems darker than usual. I can't even see my hands in front of my face.

"Wait, where's Jeremy?" Jeffrey asks. "He must still be inside—"

"I found a flashlight!" Jeremy shouts, waving it around in the air.

"SH!" I put my finger up to my mouth. "Who knows what other infected people lurk around."

Jeremy nods his head in embarrassment and walks ahead of us while lighting the dark atmosphere so we can see.

"So, what are we going to tell Counselor James once we find him?" Jeffrey whispers.

"The truth, that a crazy kid attacked me, and we locked him in the bathroom."

I'm not sure why Jeffrey asked me that. *What did he expect us to tell Counselor James?*

"Don't forget about the part where the Undead Tale ties in!" Jeremy yells from the front of our group.

I put my finger up to my mouth and Jeremy whispers, "sorry."

Jeffrey turns his attention back to me. "It doesn't sound very believable," he utters.

I raise my eyebrows. "It doesn't matter how unbelievable it sounds; we have proof right in our cabin!"

"Yeah, if no one believes us, they can just see for themselves!" Rob exclaims.

Jeffrey exhales deeply. "Yeah, I guess you're right."

I can see the counselor cabin ahead of us. The lights are still on, which is lucky for us, because it's helping light the way. I suddenly hear rustling in the woods behind us. I turn to look in the direction, but I can't see a thing (it is dark after all). Maybe it's my imagination, but I can't help but feel a little concerned. Instantly, a nervous chill goes down my spine, so I silently pray to God for our protection. I don't know how serious this is, and I'd rather be safe than sorry.

Jeremy starts fidgeting with his hands nervously. "Let's see if Counselor James is in there. If he isn't, we'll tell the other counselors what we saw."

Maybe he heard the rustling in the woods as well.

I walk up the short steps that lead to the cabin and slowly reach for the door handle. My hand starts shaking like a leaf and it's making it difficult for me to get a grip on the knob.

"Get it together Axel," I mumble.

I turn around and see the other boys lined up behind me, waiting for me to make the first move. I finally get a grip on the knob and open the door slowly. From where I'm standing, there isn't a person in sight. I can hear a faint mumbling, maybe a tv or something, but other than that, no sign of anyone.

"Uh—after you! I've seen enough horror movies to know that you should never be the first in line...or the last," Rob utters, pointing at me, then to Jeffrey behind him.

I let out a laugh, then take a deep breath. I slowly step inside the cabin. One foot quietly after the other.

82

Surprisingly it looks almost identical to our cabin. There's a small desk in the middle of the floor with a laptop and a cellphone on it, and there's a chair positioned perfectly under the desk. The only difference between our cabins is that the beds aren't bunks, but regular full-sized ones.

I take one more look around for any sign of the counselors. "I don't see anyone in here guys."

The boys slowly walk inside and observe the area.

"Where are they?" Mike asks as he steps in behind Jeffrey.

I turn my head around and wrinkle my forehead in confusion. *What is Mike doing here?*

"Oh, you finally decided to join us, huh?" Jeffrey asks.

Mike saunters around the cabin. "Just to be clear. I didn't follow you guys because I thought Axel was right." He glares at me before continuing. "I just left because that kid kept banging on the door so hard, and I couldn't get any sleep."

I roll my eyes. "Whatever, Mike."

Mike waves his hand in the air and dismisses my comment.

"Hey guys, check this out!" Jeremy shouts as he points to a box tv hanging on the ceiling. "The news is on!"

I turn my attention to the news anchor on the screen.

"Breaking news! The virus that many people thought was a hoax is real! The government did not want the public to panic, and they believed that they had everything under control, but they no longer do. This virus is getting out of hand, and many people are contracting it as we speak!"

I shake my head. "That's crazy—"

"Sh, Axel!" Mike interrupts, pointing at the television.

"We don't have enough information on how this virus came about, but all we know is that it's similar to the rabies virus. If someone contracts it, they act irrationally and non-human! A difference that we've noticed so far in comparison to the rabies virus is that they act more violent and more aggressive, and their skin and eyes change color!"

"That's just like the guy in our cabin!" Jeremy worries.

"SH!" Mike holds his finger up to his mouth.

"If someone groans, has grayish-white eyes, or tries to bite you, avoid them at all costs! DO NOT GET BIT! If

84

you get bitten, you will contract the virus, but we're still figuring out how long it takes for a person to turn. The West Coast is showing little to no cases, so, if you can, get to that side of the U.S. as soon as possible. Stay safe while the government tries to fix the issue. Good night."

The tv then goes to a commercial about insurance.

Jeffrey puts his arm around his brother. "This can't be happening."

"I told you it had something to do with that stupid virus!" I respond in frustration.

Jeremy takes his glasses off and wipes his eyes. "Yeah, you were right…"

Jeffrey sits down in a chair. "I just don't know how something like this could have happened."

"Maybe everyone's turning into monsters, because people from another planet are trying to take over, and we'll have to fight them off!" Rob announces while moving his hands in a karate motion.

I guess we're all thinking the same thing, because everyone ignores what he said as if he didn't say a word.

Jeremy starts looking around frantically. "Do you think the counselors left us?"

Jeffrey groans. "I wish I had a better answer bro, but I think they did leave. They probably heard about the outbreak and got scared."

Rob points to a window near the door. "But...their cars are still here. Why would they leave without their cars?" Jeffrey turns to Rob. "And if their cars are still here, where are they?" he gulps.

A shiver goes down my spine. I place my hands on the window and scan the vicinity, hoping to notice a counselor walking by...but no sign of anyone.

Mike stares out the window, and I notice a slight fear in his eyes. He's pretending that he's not fazed by any of this, but even the toughest person would be scared. "Honestly, I don't see why it's such a bad thing that the counselors left. We're at a camp all by ourselves!" he shouts.

I ignore his comment and look at the other guys. "Look, if we really are by ourselves, we need to get the rest of the kids at camp and bring them here."

Jeffrey nods his head. "Yeah, you're right we should..."

"AHHH!"

I hear a row of screams coming from behind the cabin.

"What was that?!" Jeremy shouts as he looks behind us.

"It sounded like it came from behind the cabin!" Jeffrey replies.

"If I'm remembering correctly, the girls' cabins are behind this one, so they might be in danger!" I shout.

Without skipping a beat, I swing the door open and race for the girls' cabins.

"Wait! We need this!"

I quickly turn my head and see Jeffrey trying to catch up. He tosses me a flashlight.

"Thanks!" I click the light on and continue running toward the cabins.

Thank goodness their cabins aren't too far from the counselors' one.

I open the first cabin door and notice two girls that look similar to the guy back at our cabin. Their eyes are a

87

grayish white, almost like life is sucked out of them. Their skin is also very pale with a green undertone and their bodies are jerking. Like how a person may flinch when they're nervous or scared…but less human, I guess.

One of the infected girls has Olivia pinned down against the wall with her vicious mouth extending toward Oli's face. Olivia is using the small amount of strength she has to hold the girl back.

I run across the cabin and push the girl off Olivia and right into the bathroom. Jeffrey runs past me and slams the bathroom door shut.

"Thanks…" Olivia bends over and places her hands on her knees, gasping for the little air she has left. "They need help!" She points to Marianne, Bella, and Selena.

Another infected girl is inches away from them and has them cornered!

"OMG! I can't die like this!" Selena screams as she squeezes Marianne's arm.

"Me neither! I want to go home!" Tears start dripping from Marianne's face onto the wooden floor.

Bella covers her face with her hands. "Help us!"

The rest of the girls race out of the cabin and scream for help.

Cowards.

Jeffrey points to one of the bunk beds. "PUSH THE BED!"

I immediately understand the assignment. I push one end of the bunk and Jeffrey pushes the other end, and the bed tips over until it leans against the wall. Thankfully, our plan works, and the infected girl is immediately trapped between the bunkbed and the wall. As soon as Marianne notices that the girl is stuck, she runs behind me, sighing in relief.

"Thanks guys!" she shouts.

Olivia puts her hand on my shoulder. "Yeah, thank you!"

I put my arms around Olivia and Marianne. "I'm just glad you guys are okay!"

"Me too! It's not like those girls from the other cabin were going to help us! They just came inside and ran away!" Olivia stomps her foot on the ground.

Jeffrey observes the girls in the distance that ran out of the cabin. "Yeah, they're definitely scaredy cats."

Bella approaches me and Jeffrey. "Thank you, Axel. And you…Jeremy, right?" she asks as a tear rolls down her cheek.

89

"Actually, I'm Jeffrey. My twin brother is Jeremy," he explains.

"Well, thank you both! My friends and I were in peril, and you both came to the rescue!" She hugs us and walks back over to Selena.

Even in a moment like this, Selena gives me a look of disapproval as she folds her arms and turns in the opposite direction.

Chapter 11:

<u>Catch Them Up</u>

We finally arrive back at the counselors' cabin and catch all the girls (from both cabins) up on what happened.

"So, the counselors abandoned us?" Selena questions.

Jeffrey folds his arms. "That's what you're worried about?"

"Look everyone! If we're going to stay out here for a few days until the government gets the outbreak under control, we need to work together," I explain.

"Days! You think it could take days?" Marianne asks while sitting on the floor.

"Don't worry, it'll be okay," I reassure while patting her on the head.

Olivia stands up. "I agree with Axel; we need to work together!"

The cabin door flies open, and a mysterious figure steps inside and takes his sunglasses off. It's none other than Counselor James.

"Counselor James, it's good to see you! You have no idea what we've been through!" I close the door behind him.

"I think I have a vague idea. The other counselors...are gone..." he slowly sits in the chair.

Wow...It seems like we've all had a rough night.

"What do you mean? Did they leave or something?" Olivia interrogates.

Everyone moves closer to him, trying to get the scoop on what happened.

"They're dead..." he mumbles.

My eyes widen. All those poor counselors...*Were they attacked by an animal? Were they infected by that virus...?*

"Oh my gosh...I need to call my uncle now!" Bella snatches her phone from out of the bin that the counselors kept our phones in.

"Did you hurt them?" Jeremy squints his eyes.

92

Counselor James grabs a bottle of water and gulps it down. "They turned into those…monster things. They were trying to kill me…I didn't know what else to do…" He lays his head on the table and sobs quietly.

I feel bad for him. I understand that he had to protect himself, but…I don't think I could hurt any of those infected people. I know they're sick, but they're still human. *At least, I think they are.*

Olivia looks out the window and points at another cabin in the distance. "We still have to tell the other boys what's going on."

So much is going on, I completely forgot about them.

"Yeah, me and Axel will go tell them," Jeffrey volunteers.

I don't know why he's volunteering me to go! I'd rather not deal with those monsters again!

"Can't someone else go this time? We just rescued the girls. What about the counselor?" I protest.

Counselor James shakes his head and places his hands over his face, continuing to whimper.

"Well, looks like he's out," I mumble.

93

Jeremy starts pacing back and forth, breathing heavily. "I guess I could go…"

Selena tilts her head to the side and stares at Jeremy with a peculiar look on her face. "Um, guys? Why's he breathing so hard?"

Jeffrey ignores Selena and hands Jeremy an inhaler.

"Thanks." He instantly presses the inhaler into his mouth.

"Do you have asthma?" I ask.

"Yeah, I do. I should be fine now."

Selena rolls her eyes. "This isn't going to be a problem, right? We don't need any liabilities."

Olivia elbows her. "Seriously Selena? That was so rude!"

"Very!" Bella frowns.

Selena puts her arms behind her back and lowers her head. "I wasn't trying to be rude!"

Don't get it twisted, Selena doesn't feel bad. She just hates disappointing Olivia. Like I mentioned before, they've been best friends for a long time, and she values Oli's opinion…To a certain extent.

"Anyway," Jeffrey stands in front of his brother like a shield. "I've got Jeremy, don't you worry about him," his voice sounding seven octaves deeper.

Selena throws her hands up in the air. "I'm just saying, someone's gotta make sure everything's alright. I wasn't trying to offend anyone."

"Yeah, whatever." Jeffrey turns back to me. "Okay. Jeremy is out of the picture. He's not doing it," he demands.

Me and Jeffrey look at Mike. He's standing in front of the tv, watching the news. He swiftly turns around and notices that we're staring at him.

"What? Why are you two staring at me?" he asks in a frustrated tone.

Jeffrey puts his hand on Mike's shoulder and lets out a sigh. "Someone needs to make sure the other guys are alright. Can you go with me?"

Mike immediately shakes his head and brushes Jeffrey's hand off his shoulder. "Nah, I'm good. Let Axel go. He said it himself; he can fight. And after that encore performance he displayed back at the cabin, I'm sure he's got this in the bag." He turns back toward the tv and continues watching.

I raise my index finger. "For your information—"

Jeremy puts his hand on my shoulder and shakes his head. He clearly doesn't want me to say anything, so I hold my tongue.

"So, who's going?" I ask.

Olivia stomps her foot on the ground. "UGH!" She snatches a flashlight off a bed and storms out of the cabin. I start to go after her, but Jeffrey stops me.

"I got this, Axel." He reaches for a flashlight and bolts out the door behind her.

....

Jeffrey finally catches up to Olivia and is slightly out of breath.

"Um, Olivia, where are you going?"

Olivia grunts as she continues to walk at a fast pace. "I'm going to check on those guys, because you all can't even decide who's going!" Her cheeks are a rosy red.

"I was going to go—"

She swings her head around. "You guys are all so selfish! One of those infected kids could have harmed some of the boys in there, and all you guys are doing is arguing about who should go!" She storms off toward the cabin.

"Wait up!" He catches up again, out of breath once more. "How are you so fast?"

She smirks. "I run track."

Taken aback, he stares in astonishment. "Woah. That takes hard work and dedication."

She turns her head and smiles. "Yeah, it does."

She slows down her pace to meet Jeffrey's, and they talk the rest of the way to the boys' cabin.

When they arrive, they walk inside the cabin and notice that all four of the boys are fast asleep.

"Lucky them. They didn't have to deal with crazy people trying to kill them," Olivia mumbles, loud enough for Jeffrey to hear.

Jeffrey nods at her comment. "Alright. Let's wake them up before something else goes wrong."

She nods her head and walks to the bunks on the opposite side of Jeffrey.

Jeffrey starts shaking one of the boys, who happens to be Weston. "You need to go to the counselors'—"

Weston opens his eyes and grabs Jeffrey's arm. "Don't touch me when I'm sleeping. Just call my name or something. You're lucky I didn't accidentally hit you," he mumbles as he releases Jeffrey's arm.

"Oh, sorry Weston." Jeffrey rubs his arm. "But you've heard about that outbreak, right?"

Weston rubs his eyes, muttering, "Yeah, I heard about it…but everyone keeps saying it's not real."

Jeffrey scratches the back of his head. "How about I just save you some time and explain everything once we head to the counselors' cabin?"

"Alright." Weston gets off the bed and picks up a bag of chips.

Olivia wakes the other boys up, and they follow Jeffrey and Olivia back to the counselors' cabin.

Chapter 12:

Time for a Plan

Olivia opens the counselors' cabin door and leads the boys inside.

"Welcome back," I announce as they make their way inside.

"Did you guys tell them what's going on?" Jeremy asks while pacing back and forth.

Jeffrey nods. "We told them on our way over here, instead of waiting."

"Yeah, so what do we do now?" Weston yawns, leaning on the wall.

"I don't know…Does anyone live in Georgia?" I ask.

Weston grabs his phone from out of the bin. "I do. I'm going to see if I can get in contact with my mom. She might be able to get here before things get too bad."

"Good idea. Everyone else, do the same if you live here," I tell them.

We all grab our phones out of the bin.

99

Olivia stands beside me and rests her head on my shoulder, mumbling, "I can't believe this is happening."

....

Weston is standing right outside the cabin door trying to reach his mom.

"Why aren't you answering your phone, Mom?!" He throws his phone on the ground out of anger.

I sigh, pacing back and forth in the small cabin.

Olivia places her hand on my back. "Axe, you're stressing everyone out."

I stand in place. "I'm sorry…I just don't know what to do. Our parents are all the way in California! How are they supposed to come all the way out here? And remember that news report I told you about? That news reporter seemed really worried. How are we supposed to get out of this, huh?" I hold my hands over my face.

Olivia puts her hands on my shoulders. "Axel, everyone's wondering the same thing…You're not alone in this."

Marianne walks over to us and nods her head. "Olivia's right. I really hope my parents come and pick me up. They're not answering their phones." She sits on the dirty wooden floor.

Jeffrey raises his hand. "You're not the only one Marianne. Jeremy and I live here too, and our parents aren't answering their phones either."

"No one cares," Selena mumbles, loud enough for everyone to hear.

Jeffrey sits up on the bed. "And no one asked your opinion."

"Yeah Selena, stop bothering people all the time…" Olivia groans.

Selena turns her back to everyone and scrolls through her phone.

Bella clears her throat. "I have to go." She quickly rushes to the door, but Olivia blocks her path.

"Why are you leaving, Bella?" Olivia inquires.

Selena darts over to them.

"My uncle lives not too far from here. I called him, and he said that he's on his way to pick me up."

101

Olivia looks at Bella frantically. "W-What about us? We're your best friends! We have to come with you!" She holds Bella's arm.

"Yeah! I know you weren't thinking about leaving US!" Selena pouts.

Bella starts rubbing her arm nervously. "O-Of course not. I wasn't thinking straight, come on!" Bella opens the door and starts running to the entrance of the camp.

Was she really going to leave Olivia and Selena behind?

"Let's go Olive!" Selena grabs her hand and pulls her toward the door.

Olivia grips the wall with her other hand, stopping Selena from pulling her any further. "Wait...I can't just leave Axel!"

I pause for a moment. *Olivia isn't thinking about herself like she usually is.*

"You can't be serious! That loser can fend for himself...Or is he just a little baby?" Selena scoffs.

"Grow up Selena. I'm tired of you always saying something about Axel." Olivia pauses and digs her foot into the wood. "I mean, sure, some of the stuff might be true—BUT it's

102

ridiculous that you're still making stupid jokes in a situation like this!" She snatches her hand from Selena's grip.

Bella notices that Olivia and Selena are still in the cabin, so she races back to them. "Are you guys coming or what?"

Olivia looks at me, then back at Bella. "Bell, Axel can come too, right? We've all known each other for a long time!"

Bella stands outside the cabin door and kicks the dirt with her shoe. "I guess—"

"You are not thinking of bringing this jerk along with us, right? He would only be a burden!" Selena yells while sinisterly smirking at me.

I ignore Selena's remark. "Come on, Bella! Is this even up for debate?"

I can't stand Selena and I'm not very fond of Bella, but I would never leave them in a dangerous situation.

Bella looks at Selena, and Selena gives her a nasty look.

She's probably trying to intimidate Bella.

"Y-You're right Selena...I'm sorry Axel..."

My eyes widen in surprise. "You've gotta be joking, Bella! Are you seriously going to just leave me like that? We've known each other for years!"

Selena puts her hand in my face. "Enough! You're not coming! Olive, are you coming?" She holds her hand out for Olivia to grab.

Olivia's face reddens. "Axel and I are family. I can't just leave him here! I wouldn't do that to my worst enemy! I'm not going anywhere with people like you!" She brushes past them and storms outside, heading toward the back of the cabin.

"Well, it's her loss. I wish she'd just come. Let's go, Bella." Selena grabs Bella's arm and pulls her away.

I watch as they both walk away from the cabin in the darkness. I ponder over whether or not I should go and speak to Olivia. She doesn't like people running behind her, but I can't just leave her alone in the woods with infected people wandering around.

I grab a flashlight, step out of the cabin, and head over to Olivia. She's sitting on the grass and staring at the ground. She looks up and notices me standing over her.

"Great…you were right about Selena and Bella. Just don't rub it in, alright?"

I scratch the back of my head and sit next to her. "You didn't have to stay here with me. I would have understood you know," I reply as I hold a flashlight in front of us.

Olivia chuckles. "You and I both know that you would never let me live that down! In ten years, you would still be mad at me for leaving you here by yourself."

We both start laughing.

"Don't worry, though. We'll be okay."

Olivia puts her hand on her face. "Are you sure about that—?"

BAM!

"What was that?" Olivia swings her head around.

I shrug my shoulders in confusion. "Not sure. Let's see what's going on." I rush toward the front of the cabin and open the door.

Everyone's staring in Weston's direction. *It's a fair assumption that's where the noise came from.*

I maneuver my way to Weston, who has his back against the wall. "What happened? We heard a loud noise."

Weston slowly picks his phone up that now has a small crack in the corner, and a larger crack resembling a lightning bolt in the middle. He slides his phone in his back pocket. "That would be my phone. I threw it on the ground because my mom is STILL not answering her phone."

Jeremy makes his way past the other kids and stands beside me, Olivia, and Weston. "Neither are my parents. Where are parents when you need them?" he laughs as he shakes his head and walks back over to his brother.

Out of nowhere, Mike dashes toward Weston excitedly. "Dude! My dad just answered his phone! He's on his way!"

Weston claps his hands. "Yes!"

"So? We can all come right?" One of the guys from the other cabin asks.

"Well, my dad only has a van that seats seven, so not everyone can go," Mike explains.

"Anyone that's left behind can stay here with me…not that I'll be much use or anything," Counselor James responds as he lays his head on the table.

"I'll go wherever you're going Axe," Olivia whispers.

Weston walks back over to me. "You weren't as bad as I thought you were going to be. You can come along if you want."

I don't know if I'm supposed to be offended or grateful.

I immediately nod my head before he can change his mind. "Uh, sure. As long as Olivia can come too."

Weston rubs his hands together. "Sure. I don't mind. Whoever fits is fine with me."

Mike shakes his head in frustration and stands between me and Weston. "Oh no! Axel is not going in my car! He can rot here for all I care, Wes!" He points his finger at me and stares into my eyes.

What is up with these people? Just because you don't like someone doesn't mean they should be left behind!

Weston slowly nods his head and places his hand on Mike's shoulder, gripping it tightly. "Oh, I thought you wouldn't mind after what happened last year…"

Sweat drips down Mike's head. "On second thought, invite anyone, I could care less!" he nervously replies and quickly shoots me a glare.

I'm glad Weston has a reputation at their school.

Weston releases Mike's shoulder from his grip, then pats him on the back in satisfaction.

Jeremy raises his index finger in the air. "Well in that case, Jeffrey and I would like to come as well!"

Marianne tugs in Weston's sleeve. "Me too…My parents aren't answering their phones, so maybe they'll be home when we get to the neighborhood!"

Weston smiles. "Of course, Marianne. I wasn't gonna leave you. My sister would kill me if I did," he jokes as he ruffles her hair. "Since you live in the same neighborhood as me, I'll walk you home when they drop us off." He then puts his arms around both Jeffrey and Jeremy. "And sure guys, you can come along, too."

Mike starts counting with his fingers. "Okay...my dad, me...Weston...and...yup! That's eight, which means someone is going to have to share a seat, but no more people can ride with me."

Rob runs over to Mike, clasping his hands together. "Wait! Please, I'm so scared...I can't be here anymore! I'll share a seat, I'll do anything!" His knees hit the floor.

Mike chuckles to himself. "You can lay in the trunk. It's not that comfortable, but—"

"I'll take it! Thank you!" Rob wipes the sweat off his forehead.

Counselor James salutes. "Well, I wish you kids the best of luck..."

I open the door as everyone makes their way out of the cabin. "You and me both."

Chapter 13:

<u>On the Road</u>

I'm sitting in the middle of the third row beside Olivia, Marianne, and Weston. Olivia's sharing a seat with Marianne, since there's eight of us in the car (not including Rob, since he's sitting in the trunk). Weston is sitting in the seat to my left, staring out the window. The row in front of us seats Jeremy and Jeffrey, and Mike is sitting in the passenger seat with his dad behind the wheel.

The car ride is quiet, which is surprising since a lot has happened so far. I turn around and spot Rob laying in the trunk while squeezing his comic book in his hands.

"You okay, man?"

He turns his head toward me and squirms in the trunk. "Y-Yeah, holding this comic book just helps me cope with the situation," he utters, shutting his eyes.

I turn back around and sit properly. "I think Rob's really scared," I whisper to Olivia (she's sitting to my right).

"Aren't we all?" She looks out the window. "It's so dark out there. Except for the dim lighting from the streetlights," she mumbles.

I glance out the window and she's right, I can barely see! Every couple of feet, there's a streetlight, but it's still difficult to see anything that's not near the lights. I can only make out a few infected people roaming the streets, arms extending toward their prey.

I look back at Olivia, and I notice her hands shaking. "Are you okay?"

I know it's a dumb question, but I don't know what else to say.

She slouches in her seat. "Yeah, I guess." She pauses for a moment and glances out the window again. "Your mom was right about us staying home. I really wish I never came."

What was I thinking? I haven't even called my parents to tell them I'm okay...!

Olivia waves her hand in front of my face. "Axel?"

I completely ignore her. Not on purpose, I'm just surprised that we forgot to reach out to our parents.

Olivia forcefully turns my face toward her. "Axel! Are you still there?"

I nod my head. "Yeah. I just realized that we haven't tried calling our parents yet!"

Olivia's eyes widen. "You're right! What were we thinking? We'll call them once we get to Weston's house."

"Yeah."

Marianne squirms in the seat she's sharing with Olivia. She's sitting between Oli and the window. "I'm so squished." She stretches her neck forward, so she can see Weston. "Will we be okay, Wes?"

Weston turns his face from the window and looks straight at her. "I don't know. But we just have to look out for each other I guess…" he sighs.

"Oh, okay." Marianne moves her neck back.

Weston turns his face back toward the window. "That was the most cliché thing I've ever said."

"Mr. Arnold, how far are we from Mitchell's Creek?" Marianne asks.

Mr. Arnold (Mike's dad) positions the rear-view mirror to reflect on Marianne's face. "Oh, not much farther now. Probably a good ten minutes," he replies, then shifts his eyes back on the road.

"Is that the neighborhood where you guys live?" I ask.

Weston leans his head on the window. "Yeah. Me and Marianne live there, but Mike lives in a different neighborhood nearby."

"Can we head to me and Jeremy's neighborhood after?" Jeffrey wonders while twisting his watch.

Mr. Arnold sighs. "Not very likely, kid. Mike and I need to make sure our other family members are okay, and we can't risk driving too much in a situation like this."

....

Mr. Arnold makes a sharp turn into Mitchell's Creek and slows the car down to a stop.

"You can stop here. Thanks for driving us. Come on guys," Weston scoots past me, and motions for Jeremy to step out of the car so he can get out.

The rest of us quietly get out of the car behind him.

"Be careful kids," Mr. Arnold whispers. He puts the gear in drive and hits the gas.

We all watch as the car fades away into the darkness.

"We should go. If those things are out here, we don't want them seeing us," I explain.

Jeremy nervously nods his head. "Y-Yeah, I'm with Axel on that one. Where's your house, Weston?"

"This way, follow me." Weston jogs while holding a flashlight, and we hastily follow behind him.

Weston stops at a brick house and opens the front door. "Come on guys!" He holds the door open, frantically waving his hand at us.

I step inside his house, with the others in toe. The first thing I notice are small wooden stairs across from the front door, leading up to the second floor.

"This is a cute house." Olivia compliments as she walks around the living space.

The twins walk inside the house and look around as well.

"Thanks, but it's not much." Weston closes the door just as Rob and Marianne run in.

The house has a nice setup. The kitchen is to my right, and there's a small table in the middle of it. The den is to my left, and there's a green loveseat with a small ottoman in the center.

The walls are covered with pictures of a Hispanic woman and two kids, one being Weston, and I'm assuming the other kid is his little sister. The girl has long black hair, a scar near her right eye, and a bucket in her hand.

"Is that your mom and little sister?" I ask, pointing to a photo of them at the beach.

"Yeah, speaking of which...! Willow? Mom? Are you guys here?" Weston starts looking around the house to find them. "I really need to find Willow. I'm sure Mom's fine."

Marianne follows Weston's lead and starts searching for his sister as well. "She's gotta be around here somewhere!"

Weston turns around and faces the rest of us. "Can you guys help me find her?"

"Yeah, of course. Don't worry, we'll find her," I reassure.

Now that we're searching for Weston's little sister, I can't help but wonder how my little brother is doing.

Weston opens a door near the kitchen.

I follow behind him and the door leads to a flight of stairs. "You think Willow's down there?"

"Yeah. She might've hidden down here." He flicks the light switch, turning on a very dim light at the bottom of the staircase.

Suddenly, I hear a faint sound in the basement. I can't quite make out the noise, but I know it's nothing good!

"Do you hear that, Weston?"

"Those things might be down there," he gulps.

I notice the fear in Weston's eyes quickly shift to determination. He walks down the basement stairs, and I follow behind him.

"What are you doing, Axe?" He stops in his tracks, nearly making me fall. "I don't need anyone to come with me."

I roll my eyes. "Look, I know you think you have something to prove—"

"I'm not trying to prove anything," he abruptly interrupts.

"What I mean is—" I clear my throat. "We get it-you're capable of handling the zombies alone—"

"*Zombies?*" Weston asks in a condescending tone.

"Well, they act like zombies, and we can't get bit by them. So, what else would you call them?"

Weston thinks for a moment, then nods his head. "I guess that makes sense. But what was your point about me being capable?" He raises his eyebrow.

"Oh right. It doesn't hurt to get help from the people around you, especially those that offer. There's no point in facing those things alone," I explain.

He sighs. "You might be right, but I can handle this…alone." He pats me on the shoulder, then continues walking down the stairs.

"Whatever, but I'll be nearby in case you need any help." I walk back up the stairs and close the door behind me.

Chapter 14:

<u>The Basement</u>

Weston cautiously walks down the stairs. With each step he takes toward the basement, his heart beats faster and louder.

"Okay, relax, I can do this," he utters calmly, trying to get his heart rate under control.

Regardless of how careful he steps, the stairs start to creak. It appears that the sound is amplified, but Weston knows that this is only in his imagination. He finally reaches the bottom step and presses his ear against the door. He can hear the sound more clearly, and it's the same sound the zombies make...*groaning.*

Weston can't make out exactly where the sound is, but he knows it's not near the door. "Hm. I guess it's not super close to the door. That's good," he mumbles to himself.

Weston prepares himself for what's behind the door. He takes a warrior stance and slowly turns the knob. As he walks in, he skims the room, but nothing's there. He takes a deep sigh of relief, stepping further into the room.

"Maybe it's just a wild animal...hopefully."

Just as Weston is about to walk out of the room, out of the shadows comes a familiar figure to him.

"Mom?!" He can see the outline of his mother, but he gets no response.

He moves closer. "Mom! You alright?" The only thing that responds is the constant sound of groaning.

His mother steps into the light and Weston finds himself face to face with what *once* was his mom but is now a zombie.

"No...You can't be one of those things!" Weston's eyes swell up as his mom eases toward him emotionlessly.

Weston recalls Jeffrey telling him that he can't get bit by the zombies, because he'll turn into one of those things. His mom races toward him and grabs his hand, pulling it toward her mouth.

Weston forcefully pushes his mom back and turns to run out of the room, but he trips on an old paint can and hits his head hard on the ground.

BAM!

119

"Ouch…" He rubs his forehead.

Just as his mom is inches away from biting him, a young girl hits her with a piece of plywood, and the zombie falls to the ground.

Weston turns behind him and sees a girl around the age of ten, tossing the plywood to the ground.

"WILLOW!" Weston pulls his sister in for a hug. "You're okay!"

"We can continue this family reunion later, come on!" She grabs Weston's hand and pulls him out of the basement, forgetting to close the metal door at the foot of the stairs.

"Hurry, Wes!" She runs up the steps, quickly pulling Weston up them.

She pushes the door at the top of the stairs open and forcefully shuts it back and locks it in the process.

Chapter 15:

<u>Check on Everyone</u>

I swing my head around, wondering what all the commotion is about. I notice Weston and a little girl standing beside him. The girl looks just like his sister in the photo mantled on the wall, so that must be her!

"What happened? Are you guys alright?" I ask.

Willow clears her throat. "Well, our mom—"

Weston quickly covers his sister's mouth. "It took me so long, because I was making sure there were no zombie things down there. Turns out it was just Willow," he utters as he pulls his sister closer to him.

"You're okay, Willow!" Marianne hugs her tightly.

"Hey Marianne…" Willow cuts her eyes at Weston as she hugs her.

I extend my hand. "Hi Willow. I'm glad to know you're okay."

Willow shakes my hand, then looks up at Weston with a curious look. "Who are all of these people?"

Weston places one hand on Willow's shoulder. "Oh! This is Axel. You probably won't like him at first, but he grows on you."

I roll my eyes. "Same for your brother, except it takes a REALLY long time to get use to his annoying tendencies."

Willow giggles.

"I'm Olivia, Axel's best friend."

Rob smiles. "And I'm Rob!"

Jeffrey waves. "I'm Jeffrey, and this is my twin brother, Jeremy."

"Wow! You found quite the bunch didn't ya, Weston?" Willow pinches Weston's arm.

"Yeah, they're alright I guess."

"So, why did you guys come up here with frightened faces?" I wonder.

Sweat starts dripping from Weston's forehead (I'm not sure why). "We weren't afraid! I was just...super excited to tell you guys that I found her!" He smiles nervously.

Unsure whether he's telling the truth or not, I shrug my shoulders. "Well, I'm glad to know that you guys are alright."

Jeremy raises his hand up like he just thought of something. "Wait, but that doesn't explain why Willow was looking super nervous?" He rubs his chin with his hand.

Weston scratches the back of his head. "So many questions with many little answers! Anyway, who's tired? I'm really tired!" He nervously responds while fake yawning.

"I have to agree with you. I'm tired too, since those zombie-things woke us up," Olivia groans.

Jeremy yawns. "Yeah, it doesn't take a rocket scientist to figure out we need rest after a horrific night."

"We need something to eat, too..." Marianne holds her stomach.

"There's some food in the fridge. Weston and I can fix some eggs," Willow offers as she opens the small refrigerator.

"You guys can try to relax while we fix the food. There's three bedrooms upstairs, and there's a chair in the master bedroom," Weston explains as he walks into the kitchen.

"Thanks guys." I make my way over to Olivia. "Let's try to call our parents upstairs."

Olivia nods her head, and we head into one of the bedrooms upstairs.

The room has a full-sized bed in the center with a dresser across from it. I notice a photo of Weston holding a football neatly placed on a nightstand next to the bed.

"We've had a pretty stressful night, huh?" Olivia sighs as she sits down on the bed.

"Yeah, one for the record books." I turn my phone on and click on my mom's contact. I impatiently wait for her to pick up, but I get a busy signal instead.

Olivia tries to call her parents, but the same thing happens. "Seems like everyone's calling their loved ones right now," she sighs.

I lay on the bed. "Maybe we'll be able to call them in the morning?"

"Maybe…" She squeezes a pillow.

"I really wish I could hug August right now…I can't even imagine what he's going through. I'm way older than him, and I'm barely handling this." I stare at the ceiling.

Olivia puts her hand on my shoulder. "Well, the news said that the West Coast isn't as bad as the East Coast, so he might not realize what's going on right now."

"Maybe."

"Well, I should get ready for bed. Goodnight, Axe." She gets off the bed and closes the door behind her.

....

I head out of the bedroom and knock on the door across from me. *I should talk to everyone before I head to bed.*

The door opens and Rob's smile greets me. "Hey Axel! Come in!" He opens the door wider, and I enter the room.

In the room, there's a large queen-sized bed with a nightstand next to it. There's also a chair in a corner near a

125

window, with photos of Willow and Weston throughout the room.

"These are nice pictures, right?" Rob looks in awe.

I point at a photo of Weston catching a football in mid-air. "Yeah. Seems like Weston's good at football."

Rob takes a seat in the chair. "Seems like it."

"So," I sit on the floor. "I bet you're scared. I know I am."

Rob leans back in the chair. "Very. I know I may come across as a goofy guy that doesn't understand what's going on, but when I'm nervous, I tend to relate real life to the comics and cartoons I watch. I know it may sound silly, but it helps me cope with different situations."

"Almost like a defense mechanism?"

Rob smiles. "Exactly."

That makes sense. I know when Olivia's stressed or nervous, she tends to get angry or frustrated. But when I'm nervous or stressed, I try to analyze the situation and remain calm (most of the time).

"What about before this apocalypse happened?" I ask.

"An apocalypse? Reminds me of a comic I once read." He laughs. "But before "this" happened, I'd get nervous around people and automatically talk about my comics, even if people thought I was weird." He stares at the ground.

"What comics do you like to read?"

His face lights up. "There's this comic called, Origin, and it's so good! It's an adventure book about a girl with superpowers. Rumor has it, it's actually a true story, but there's no evidence to back up the claim," he shrugs his shoulders, unsure if the last part is true.

"I've never heard of that comic, probably because I don't really read them."

"Well, they have a novel version of it too, so maybe once this is over you could read it?"

I nod my head. I usually don't read much of anything, unless it's for school, but maybe that book is worth reading.

"Sure, why not?" I stand up and reach for the door handle. "I've enjoyed your company, but I'm gonna talk to everyone else before I head to bed."

Rob stretches his arms. "Okay, I'll see you around."

I leave Rob's room and head down the stairs. I'm pretty sure Jeremy and Jeffrey are in the den.

Yup. I was right. Jeffrey's sitting on the couch, his back facing me. "Hey Jeff." I walk into the den and sit down beside him.

Jeffrey lifts his head. "Hey."

"Where's Jeremy?"

Jeffrey points to Jeremy, who's fast asleep on the rug. "He fell asleep not too long ago." He grabs a magazine off the small table in front of the couch. He begins flipping the pages and stops on one. "Look at this!"

He turns the magazine around, and I see a photo of a man holding a pistol in one hand and a med-kit in the other. I squint my eyes and read the title.

Are you ready for the apocalypse? Keep reading this to see if you've got what it takes to survive!

He turns the magazine back around. "If only I read this a day earlier." He bursts into laughter.

"Tell me about it. What does the page say anyway?"

Jeffrey skims through the page and lets out another laugh. "I guess we have no hope. Listen to this," he holds the magazine up. "The only way to survive an apocalypse is to fly to another country in hopes that they're not dealing with the same thing. Otherwise, you're done for!"

"Wow…I guess we should give up now!" I chuckle.

"Exactly." His face turns serious. "That's not true though, right?"

I rub my forehead. "I'm not sure…"

"So, you think we're done for?" Jeffrey lets out a deep sigh.

"I'm not sure what to think." I grab a water bottle that's on the table and gulp it down.

"Well, I don't know about anybody else, but Jeremy and I will be okay," he replies with determination.

"We all will be."

Jeffrey looks at me and raises his eyebrows. "Do you actually believe that?"

I stare at the ground for a moment before responding. "I don't know."

Chapter 16:

<u>The Truth</u>

Weston scrambles a few eggs in a pan, while Willow cooks some bacon.

"Why did you lie to your friends?" Willow inquires as she flips the bacon.

"Because, if they found out about Mom being down there, they would have killed her or thrown her out," Weston explains while grabbing an ice pack from the freezer.

Willow nods as she sprays butter on the bacon.

"Also," he turns to her. "How did you know I was down there?"

She clears her throat. "I was hiding upstairs in my closet when I heard you calling my name. I wanted to come out, but I was just so scared that you'd turn into a zombie too, so I stayed hidden." She flips a few pieces of bacon. "But then I overheard your friends saying that you went in the basement, and I knew I had to save you before it was too late."

130

Weston puts his hand on her shoulder. "Thank you."

"You're welcome. I knew your friends would only slow me down, so I snuck past them and went in the basement alone," she finishes.

He puts an icepack on his head. "How did Mom get down there anyway?"

Willow starts fidgeting with her hands. "Yesterday morning, I was sleeping when I heard screaming downstairs," she swallows. "I quickly hurried down to see what was going on, and I couldn't believe that Mom was getting bit by a zombie!"

She takes a deep breath. "With all Mom's might, she pushed the zombie out of the house and locked herself in the basement. She didn't want to hurt me…" Willow covers her face with her hands.

Weston hugs his sister. "It's okay Willow. You don't have to talk about it." He holds back tears himself.

....

131

I walk into the kitchen and notice that both Weston and Willow are visibly upset.

"You guys alright?"

Willow wipes her tears with her shirt and Weston clears his throat.

"Yeah, we're good. She's just really upset about the outbreak." Weston wipes the sweat trickling down his forehead.

"Oh, I guess that makes sense." I put my hand on Willow's shoulder. "It's going to be alright, Willow. Your brother will look out for you. Don't you worry," I smile and sit at the kitchen table.

"Thanks...I'm just going to grab this piece of bacon and head to bed. Goodnight." She grabs the bacon and quickly leaves the room.

Weston grabs the spatula off the counter and continues scrambling the eggs.

"You seem like a good older brother." I tell him as I watch him cook.

Weston laughs and shakes his head. "Oh? You can just tell when someone's a good older sibling based on one encounter you've witnessed?" he responds with sarcasm in his voice.

I laugh to myself. *Weston is always on the defense.*

"I'm an older brother too, so I can tell. You don't always have to respond sarcastically or with an attitude."

Weston turns to me and leans his hands on the table. "You don't know me, Axel, so don't act like you do," he snaps as he turns back toward the food.

"Well, first impressions say it all and your impression hasn't been the best. Aside from the way you treat Willow," I mumble.

Weston turns the stove off and shakes his head once more. "I may not be as friendly as you, but I still have good qualities, whether people notice or not, and I could care less if they do. I have one goal and one goal only, and that's to look out for Willow. Making good impressions on you guys isn't something I'm focused on." He scoops some eggs on a plate and leaves the kitchen without another word.

Chapter 17:

Help is Near

I slowly open my eyes. I didn't sleep well at all, which, aside from the flesh-eating monster situation, was probably due to the disagreement that Weston and I had in the kitchen last night. I just kinda feel bad about it.

Aside from the compliment about being a good older brother, he's right about the things I said. I don't really know him that well, and it was rude of me to make accusations based on petty confrontations that took place when we were at camp. I should probably get out of bed though, as much as I'd rather not.

I look at the alarm clock on the nightstand.

"1:35 p.m."

I'm not sure what time it was when I went to sleep, but I should feel a lot more refreshed than I do right now. As I stand up and open the bedroom door, my stomach begins to growl. I'm starting to regret that I ate so little last night. I slowly make my way down the stairs and notice that everyone is sitting around the television in the living room.

"You think we could make it there?" Rob asks with hope in his eyes.

"Maybe, but isn't everyone else going to head there? Is it worth the risk?" Weston wonders.

"What's worth the risk?" I walk in the living room, and everyone looks at me.

"Oh, I thought you were already down here," Jeffrey utters.

I shrug. "So, what are you guys talking about?"

"Oh," Jeremy starts, "we were watching the local news, and apparently the mayor wants everyone to go to the courthouse."

I tilt my head. "The courthouse? Why the courthouse?"

Jeffrey leans forward. "They're setting up a safe zone there."

"It's a start, but they said if things don't get better, they'll take further measures to protect the citizens here in Georgia," Olivia finishes.

"What if there's not enough room for everyone to come? A lot of people live here," I explain.

Everyone pauses for a moment, then Weston breaks the silence.

"I have to protect my sister, and if that means taking that risk, then I guess I'll take it." He opens a closet door and pulls out a pistol.

"Woah! Do you really think that's necessary?" Jeffrey stares at him in disbelief.

Weston grabs a holster out of the closet as well. "Yes, it is necessary! You heard the news, if you get bit, you're done for! I can't risk me or Willow getting hurt!" He puts the pistol in the holster and clips the holster to his waistband.

"But those things are still people!" Marianne protests.

Willow interjects. "It's either kill or be killed. My brother's right, if we try to act like those things are still our loved ones, then we will very well become one, too." Willow looks at Weston.

"Honestly, you do what you want, Weston. Me on the other hand won't be killing anyone," Jeremy replies with determination.

I glance at Jeremy, then Weston.

Only one choice will keep me alive.

Back at the cabin, I was shocked that Counselor James hurt the counselors when they turned. Now, I understand why he did it. *To protect himself.*

I take a deep breath. "Well, I agree with Weston. I have to protect those that I care about. I have a little brother waiting for me back home, and I'm going to make it back to him in one piece. I'd rather not hurt anyone, but I will defend myself if necessary."

Olivia shoots me a disapproving look.

Weston puts his hand on my shoulder. "Good. At least I know you'll survive."

Good thing he's not holding a grudge from last night.

"I agree," Rob utters. "Kind of."

"I guess you guys have your values, and I have mine," Olivia replies as she flips her hair. "But anyway," she changes the subject, "you guys ready to go?"

"Yeah, let's go," Rob responds.

Marianne tugs on Weston's sleeve. "Wait! Can I go to my house now? I want to make sure my family is okay!"

Weston nods his head. "Yeah, I'll walk you there, then we'll use my mom's car to head to the courthouse."

137

Olivia is eager to lead the charge to the courthouse. She grabs the car key on the table and reaches for the front door handle.

BOOM!

A loud noise erupts behind us, and a chill goes down my spine.

"What was that...?" I turn around to see what all the commotion is about. To my horror, a zombie broke the basement door, and her lifeless body is making its way toward us!

"ZOMBIE!" I yell. I could barely get the word out, but as soon as I said it, Olivia grabs Marianne's hand and swings the front door open, Jeffrey and Jeremy are not far behind.

I snatch the gun from Weston's holster and aim it at the zombie.

"No!" Weston tries to take the gun from me.

"What are you doing, give it back!"

"You're not going to kill her!" he yells.

We frantically try to pull the gun from each other's grip.

"AH!" Willow screams.

I turn around and the zombie is inches away from Willow!

"WILLOW!" Weston snatches the gun from my hand and aims it at the zombie and pulls the trigger…But to our horror, no bullets come out.

"Oh gosh…" Weston stares at Willow and both of their eyes lock on one another.

The zombie grabs Willow's arm and pulls her hand toward her mouth. Weston takes off running towards her, but I already know by the time he gets to her, it'll be too late.

As the zombie's teeth are centimeters from Willow's arm, Rob is the only one close enough to save her, and surprisingly, he jumps into action! He pulls her arm from the zombie's grip. But when he moves her arm, the zombie bites his instead!

"AHH! HELP!" Rob screams, as the zombie sinks her teeth into his arm.

"Think!" I notice a broom leaning on the wall by the front door. "I can use that!" I snatch the broom and hold the bristle side up. I charge toward the zombie and, with all my might, push her back down the basement stairs.

BAM!

139

I look over the stairs and the zombie isn't moving an inch. I exhale deeply. Thank goodness that's over…I look at Rob, and he's staring at his arm in disbelief.

"A-Are you okay...?" I ask, my voice cracking as I stare at the bite on Rob's arm.

"No...no...no…" Rob mumbles. "This wasn't supposed to happen."

"I don't know what to say…" Weston's eyes are welling up with tears, but he's refusing to let any fall.

"T-Thank y-you…" Willow reaches to hug Rob, but Weston pulls her back before she reaches him.

"We don't know how long it takes before he turns—"

I clench my fists. "He just saved your sister's life, and all you can think about is the bite!" I shout. "Let's go, Rob!"

Rob stares at the floor as I lead him outside the house.

As I step outside with Rob, I'm met by three guys with guns in their hands.

Two of the men are Caucasian, while the other one is Hispanic. From a distance, they look like average guys, but up close you can see the anger and evil that's inside.

"You didn't tell me that there were more of you?" One of the white guys utter, pointing his gun at me and Rob.

"What do you want?" Olivia objects.

Marianne squirms.

"Well, I'm sure you all heard that everyone needs to head to the courthouse. That's where everyone will be safe!" The man answers.

"Yeah, Bobby's right, and we need to get there fast, so we're going to take this car!" the Hispanic man finishes, as he points to the key in Olivia's hand.

"You can't just take it; we should be helping each other!" I yell.

The third man laughs hysterically at my comment. "What fairytale are you living in kid? We're trying to help ourselves—"

"How about you mess with someone your own size?" A man with a bandana around his mouth and a bow in his hand approaches us.

The three men laugh again.

"I'm so scared! A loner with a bow! Newsflash, we have guns!" The man named Bobby provokes.

The mysterious man scratches his head and chuckles at his comment. "Come 'on man, give these kids a break. We're supposed to be helping each other, not tearing each other down. Just let them be on their way." He cracks his neck from side to side.

The man named Bobby cracks his knuckles. "How about you mind your own business and get lost alright—"

Before he can finish, the mysterious man shoots an arrow right in his leg.

Bobby grabs his leg in agony. "AHHH!" And he collapses to the ground.

"You're going to regret that!" The other white man shouts. He raises his gun, but the mysterious man shoots an arrow in his leg before he could pull the trigger.

"AHH!"

The Hispanic man drops his gun and takes off running toward the woods.

Thank goodness those psychos are gone.

We all sigh in relief, knowing that those guys can't mess with us anymore.

"Thanks for your help, sir," Jeffrey sighs in relief.

Olivia shakes the man's hand. "Thank you…It was violent but thank you."

"Yeah, thanks," I tell him as I turn my back on the two men.

"No problem. No one should mess with kids, especially in unprecedented times such as this. I'd rather have a conversation, but it didn't seem like those guys were gonna negotiate."

"Probably not," Jeremy admits.

Weston swings the front door open and makes his way to us. "Thanks for saving them, sir."

"You're welcome, but you guys should get going. Who knows how many more psychos are around here like those poor saps?" He looks down at the men, who are now passed out.

I nod. "Yeah, you're right, thanks again."

"Wait, what's your name, sir?" Jeremy looks at him.

"Oh—you can call me Reese."

I let out a deep sigh.

Reese raises his eyebrow. "Sorry my name offends you, kid."

I shake my hands. "No, it's not that. My dad's name was Reese."

Reese scratches his chin. "Well, I can promise you that I'm not him," he laughs.

I shake my head. "Yeah, I know that much."

Every time I hear this guy's name, it's gonna remind me of the permanent pain in my chest anytime I think of my dad.

Weston interrupts. "Anyway, we should get going, guys. Thanks again Reese." He sits in the driver seat of the SUV while Olivia hops in the passenger seat.

Willow sits in the middle row with Jeremy and Jeffrey, and Rob lays in the trunk.

"Come on, Axel! There's room for you in the third row," Weston yells.

"Okay...!"

I feel like we're forgetting someone. Olivia's in the car, the twins, Rob...Wait a sec... where's Marianne?!

"Is Marianne in the car?" I ask.

Weston looks in the rearview mirror. "No. I thought she was with you, Olivia!" Weston turns to her.

Olivia starts biting her bottom lip. "No! She was beside me when I came out of the house, but not after that!"

Reese leans his back on the car. "I saw a little girl running toward a red brick house, so maybe that's the girl you all are looking for?"

"Yeah, that's probably her! But we don't have time to look for her, she'll probably be fine!" Olivia groans.

Weston takes a deep breath. "I want to look for Marianne, but we have to go to the courthouse," he responds.

Willow leans forward. "Yeah, my brother's right. We have to get to safety, even if it means leaving my best friend."

I understand what they're saying, but we can't just leave Marianne out here.

I look at the brick house in the distance. "Fine, you guys can go ahead. I'll look for her."

Olivia's eyes widen. "No way, Axel! We stick together!"

"Oli, I can't just leave her here. She might need help."

Olivia opens the car door and runs up to me. "Then I'm coming with you!" she shouts emphatically.

I shake my head. "No, I don't want to put you in any danger. Just head to the courthouse with them."

Olivia's usually not one to back down, but hopefully she listens to me this time.

Olivia reluctantly agrees. "Fine, but if anything happens to you, I'll never listen to you again." Her voice cracks.

"God will look out for me. I'll be fine," I reassure.

At the sound of that, her shoulders relax, and she hops back in the car.

Weston sticks his hand out of the window. "We'll scope the place out, then we'll come back and pick you up, okay?"

"Alright, just be careful!" I wave as Weston starts the SUV up and pulls off.

"Come on, let's find that girl of yours." Reese pats me on the back and starts leading the way. "I caught your name was Axel?"

"Yeah."

146

"Hm, pretty cool name." He continues walking.

"Thanks, my mom named me after one of her favorite characters…" I chuckle as I start thinking about Mom.

Reese waves his hand in front of my face. "Axel? You lost in thought?"

"Uh, yeah, just thinking about my mom…"

I trail off as I hear the same sound that's been haunting us…*groaning.* Which only means one thing: zombies. I look over my shoulder and see at least ten zombies running toward us.

I start walking forward, quickening my pace. "Reese…There's zombies behind us," I mumble as the words barely come out.

Reese turns around and his eyes widen. "Uh-oh. I forgot sound attracts those things. I shouldn't have shot those guys with the arrows. They screamed too loud."

I adjust my pace to a jog. "Sound attracts them?" I inquire.

"Yeah, but Biology lesson later." He pulls a gun out of his holster and pulls the trigger, but no bullets come out. "Dang it!"

147

"I'm having back luck with guns," I mumble to myself.

"They're running faster!" Reese shouts as he races past me.

I sprint after him. "Wait for me!"

Reese frantically looks around. "We need to find another car! We'll be able to get away from them if we do!"

I notice a truck in the driveway of a house nearby. "This way Reese!" I race to the driver's side and pull the handle, and to my amazement, it opens! I smile in relief and hop inside.

Reese opens the passenger door and gets in. "Hopefully we can drive around for a while and come back for your friend."

"Why can't we just go inside a house? I ask him.

"If we go inside a house, we don't know what's in there, and it's only a matter of time before they get inside. But in a car, we can keep driving and they'll eventually stop chasing us. I hope."

BANG!

A zombie starts hitting my window as hard as it can!

"It's going to break the window," Reese mumbles under his breath.

Something shiny in the cupholder catches my eye. "What is that?" I reach my hand for the object and realize that it's a key fob for the truck!

Reese stares in disbelief. "Looks like the bad luck is behind us. Now, let's get out of here!"

I turn the car on and hit the gas!

Reese puts his seatbelt on and watches as the zombies try to catch up to the truck. "Nice job."

I nod as I try to focus on the road. "Thanks, but we're not safe yet. We'll be okay once we get out of the neighborhood." I look in the rearview mirror and observe the zombies chasing the truck.

"AXEL, WATCH OUT!" Reese shouts.

I shift my eyes back on the road, and a zombie is standing in the middle of it.

Reese puts his hands on the dashboard. "WE'RE GONNA HIT IT!"

I squint my eyes and with all my might, I swerve the truck to the left in hopes of dodging the zombie, but to my horror, the truck slams into a house…and everything goes black.

Chapter 18:

<u>Time to Move</u>

I slowly grow conscious. *Did I pass out?* I touch the back of my head, and a sharp pain travels through my skull. "Oww…" I quickly snatch my hand back.

I look around. The hood of the car is partially inside the house I crashed into. Hopefully no one was harmed (aside from me and Reese). I catch a whiff of smoke, which I soon realize came from the airbag.

"It smells awful." I push the airbag out of my face and glance at the passenger seat. Thankfully it deployed for the driver and passenger sides (which probably saved my life).

Wait, where's Reese?

I take another look at the passenger seat, and he's not there. He *has to be around here somewhere.* My thoughts are interrupted by the sound of zombies behind the truck.

As I'm assessing the situation, I remember Reese telling me that sound attracts zombies.

151

"Uh-oh. I forgot sound attracts those things. I shouldn't have shot those guys with the arrows. They screamed too loud."

If screaming alerted the zombies, then the car smashing into a house DEFINITELY got their attention. I should get out of here as soon as possible and think about Reese later. I can't help him if I'm dead.

With my hand shaking, I adjust the rearview mirror, so I can see behind me. Zombies are making their way toward the truck, giving me only a few seconds to think of a way out of here!

Adrenaline starts kicking in, and now I can barely feel the pain I was in. I look down and find a gun on the floor of the truck. I grab it and slide it in my pocket. "Now to get out of here."

I pull the handle on the door but to no avail, it's jammed. Time is running out, so I grab the gun and aim it at the window.

POW!

Thank goodness whoever owned this truck had a gun inside.

I instinctively cover my ears. *I didn't realize it was gonna be so loud.* I take my seatbelt off and try to climb out of the car, when suddenly a zombie breaks the passenger window and grabs my leg!

I use my right leg and kick the zombie with all my strength, but it barely leaves a mark. "LET ME GO!" I quickly point the gun at the zombie's arm and shoot.

POW!

To my dismay the zombie's arm comes flying off, and he starts pulling me with his other hand!

That's disgusting.

"Why aren't you dead?!" With all my might, I scramble towards the window, but I feel his teeth sink into my shoe!

"NO!" I kick the zombie again and he releases his grip on me, and I scramble out of the truck as fast as I can and fall flat on my face.

"Ouch." Seems the adrenaline was the only reason I was able to escape the zombie. My whole body is in agony, which probably has a lot to do with the accident.

I use the truck as leverage and get on my feet. Sharp pains go up and down my body as I struggle to stand. I glance

153

back at the car to make sure the zombie isn't coming for a round two. But as I look inside, I realize pieces of glass from the window stuck the zombie and killed it.

"Finally. I guess I kicked it right into a pile of glass."

I limp across the pavement and head to the house Reese told me he saw Marianne enter. As I approach the front door of the home, I contemplate on whether I should knock or not.

I reach for the knob and open the door. "Courtesy went out the window when people started biting each other." As I step inside the house, I lock the door behind me.

The silence is unnerving. Another sharp pain shoots through my body, and my body involuntarily buckles to the ground in hopes of sheltering the pain. I don't care if someone's in here or not, I need rest. I ease forward and take a seat on a couch that's in the middle of the den. Through all the pain, I almost forgot that the zombie bit my shoe, but hopefully the bite didn't go through…

As I'm slowly sliding my shoe off, I hear a creak behind me.

Please don't be a zombie.

I swiftly swing my head around and to my surprise, Marianne is peaking behind a wall.

"A-Axel?" Marianne whispers, looking frightened.

My mood lightens as she approaches me. "Hey Marianne, I'm glad to know you're okay."

Out of the shadows come three new faces. A man with a bald head and black glasses, a woman with short red hair, and a little boy, no older than three.

Marianne wraps her arms around the little boy. "Me too! And guess what? I found my family!"

I force a smile. "That's good," while lifting my thumb up.

The woman, who I assume is Marianne's mom, takes a seat beside me. "Marianne told us that you kids looked out for her. Thank you for being nice to our daughter."

Marianne's dad (I assume) puts a hand on the woman's shoulder. "Yes, thank you. When we went to the camp a few hours ago, it was infested with those zombie things. We thought the worst, but then Marianne knocked on the door." A tear rolls down his cheek as he looks at Marianne.

Infested? I guess that means the rest of the kids might have turned...

155

I tune them out for a moment. I wanna be happy for them, but the uncertainty of being bit is driving me crazy. So, I slowly remove my sock and look for any trace of a zombie bite.

"I wasn't bit! Oh, thank you God!" A weight is lifted off my shoulders.

Marianne stares at me in confusion. "You thought you were bit?" She wrinkles her forehead.

I nod. "Yeah, while I was looking for you, a zombie bit my shoe. But thank goodness the bite didn't go through.

Marianne lowers her head. "I'm so sorry. I didn't know you were looking for me...If you were really bit, it would've been my fault." She stares at the ground.

I put my shoe back on. "Don't be sad! I'm okay, and that's all that matters. By the way, our friends will be here soon, and then we'll head to the courthouse."

Marianne's dad rubs the back of his head. "Actually," he clears his throat, "we won't be going there."

My eyes widen. "What? But the news said to head there!"

"I know, but a lot of people will be there, and that's a risk we're not willing to take." He puts his arms around his kids.

I hold my side. "I get it."

Marianne leans in and hugs me. "I'll be okay, and so will you!"

I lean back on the couch. "Yeah, we will." I turn my attention to her parents. "Is it okay if I stay here until my friends pick me up?"

Marianne's mom stands up and nods excitedly. "Of course! You can get some rest on the couch. We'll let you know when we see your friends coming back."

"Thanks, but I'm too anxious to sleep even if I wanted to. If they're not back in an hour, I'm going to go to the courthouse myself," I explain, while grabbing a magazine from off the glass table.

Marianne's dad hands me antibiotic ointment, rubbing alcohol, and a couple of gauze. "You have cuts and bruises all over your face and arms! Use these to patch yourself up."

"Thanks! Can I use your bathroom to bandage myself up?"

He points to a door down the hall. "There's the bathroom right there. There's also some band-aids in there if you need it."

I nod and make my way into the bathroom and close the door. "Gosh, I do have a lot of cuts on my face. At least they're not deep." I stare at my reflection in the mirror and pour the rubbing alcohol on the gauze. "Here comes the fun part." I dab the gauze on my cuts, and a stinging sensation follows.

"Ow."

Now that I cleaned my cuts, I grab the ointment and apply that on the wounds. "Where are those band-aids he was talking about?" I spot the band-aids on the counter and put them on my face and arms.

"I guess today could've gone worse." As I finish, another sharp pain shoots down my body, and as a result, I bend down and grip myself in agony.

The pain finally subsides, and I make my way out of the bathroom. I'm mindful to move carefully, ensuring I do not encourage another round of pain with any sudden movement. I join the others in the den and lay on the couch.

"Do you guys have any pain medicine? I got into a car accident earlier."

158

Marianne's mom pulls some aspirin from a drawer and hands it to me. Wow, you've been through a lot. Here, take this!"

I take two pills. "Thanks."

I can't believe this is really happening. Zombies are roaming the streets, waiting to devour anything in their paths. Something about this just doesn't add up, though. Why didn't the zombie die when I shot his arm? Can they not feel pain when they're in that state? Maybe it's just like the movies...or not. So many questions with very little answers.

Chapter 19:

<u>Regrouping</u>

I watch the tenth episode of Family Tunes and look out the window. *Good. I can't see any zombies in sight.* I look at Marianne; she's fast asleep on the other side of the couch.

"We'll get through this, somehow." I place a cover over her.

Her brother's sitting on the floor while watching television, giggling at all the corny lines on the cartoon.

"I used to think this was funny too." I ease off the couch and look out the window again. Now there are a few zombies wandering outside.

Marianne wakes up and rubs her eyes. "How many are out there?"

"Not enough to worry about. I'll be fine." I close the blinds.

She hops off the couch. "How do you feel?"

To be honest, I feel better than I did a few hours ago, but I still don't feel that great. No broken or sprained bones, but I was JUST in a car accident, so I'm still in pain. *I'm probably going to downplay it a bit though.*

"The pain's subsiding." In an effort to change the subject, I walk to the door. "I should head out now."

"During the day?"

"Best time, right? I can see my surroundings. Besides, the rest of the group should be back any minute."

Marianne slouches. "Okay..."

I grab my gun and look in the magazine that holds the bullets. "None...There could still be a bullet in the chamber... hopefully."

Marianne shrugs her shoulders. "I'm just going to pretend I know what you're talking about." She mumbles as she brushes her hair. "So, this is it? You're really leaving?"

"Yeah. I've gotta look out for my family, and yours will look out for you. Don't worry, God will protect us."

"What if I never see you again?"

I bend down, so we meet eye to eye. "Even if we never cross paths, I'll never forget you, Marianne."

Her mother makes her way into the den. "You know you don't have to leave if you don't want to, right?"

I reach for the doorknob on the front door. "I know, but I have to make sure my mom, little brother, and stepdad are okay." I open the front door and step outside before they try to convince me any further.

Marianne waves at me. "Bye Axel! I'll never forget you either!" She squeezes her mom's hand and closes the door.

I can't believe it. I'm probably never going to see Marianne again. The craziest part about it all is that I'll never know if she'll be okay or not. Maybe that's for the best, though. If something did happen to her, I'd rather not know.

I walk over to the truck that I crashed and try to get it started again (which I highly doubt will happen). To my surprise (not really), the car doesn't start. It won't even turn over. "Great. Looks like I'm walking," I utter, while dragging my feet across the driveway.

I'm glad I took some aspirin, because if I was in the same pain that I was in earlier, I wouldn't be able to walk. As I make my way out of the neighborhood, I notice a zombie in the middle of the road, facing the other direction.

162

"Okay...It doesn't see me yet." I start creeping backwards, hoping it won't notice me.

I continue tiptoeing away from the zombie, not taking my eyes off it for one second, when suddenly, I trip on something.

BAM!

I fall flat on my back and hit my head on the road. "Ouch."

If the car crash didn't leave a mark, this definitely did. As I rub the back of my head, I notice a pipe laying on the ground next to me (which is probably what I tripped over).

I look back up in hopes that the zombie didn't hear me fall...But of course, it did.

He turns his crooked neck around and stares straight at me. He has a salt and pepper beard with wrinkles all over his face and pale skin. Before he turned crazy, he probably had a good life, but now he's just a flesh-eating creature, waiting to devour everything around him.

He begins to move his bony legs across the road, one step a little faster than the other. I watch in horror as the zombie is now practically running straight for me!

"Oh great! Can these things give me a break?" I get on my feet and grab the pipe. As the zombie is inches away from me, I swing the pipe and clothesline him.

The zombie hits the ground with a big BOOM! But to my surprise, he gets right back up. He lets out a loud growl and starts racing after me again, but I hit his legs with the pipe, and he goes face-first on the ground.

"Finally!"

While he's down, I run as fast as I can (ignoring the pain in my legs) past it. I can hear the zombie running behind me, but I refuse to get distracted. "This one's relentless."

As soon as the words slip out, I hear a loud bang behind me. I immediately turn around and surprisingly, the zombie is laying on the ground, lifeless, with Weston right next to it.

"You're welcome," he smirks as he spins a gun in his hand.

I toss the pipe on the ground and sigh in relief. "Thanks. I don't know how much longer I could've ran."

Weston leans his back on a pole. "Probably not that long." He chuckles. "You're lucky I found a bullet at the courthouse. You would've been dead if I didn't."

Before I can respond, I feel a hand touch my shoulder.

"Axel, are you okay?" The voice cracks.

I'd know that voice anywhere. It's Olivia.

I look over my shoulder. *Yup, it's her.* "Yeah, mostly."

She stares at me wide-eyed. "Why do you have so many bruises and band-aids on your face? What did you do?" She taps her foot on the ground (like a parent would).

If I tell her the full story, she'll just go into panic mode. *"I shouldn't have left you! I can't believe you got hurt!"* She'll just start blaming herself...or me, which is not good for anyone.

I clear my throat as I think of an excuse to come up with. "I didn't really get hurt. You worry too much," I reply in a nonchalant tone.

Olivia puts her hands on her hips. "I know you're hiding something Axel Skylark, but I'll let it slide *this* time." She

165

points her finger at me in irritation but soon changes her mood to relief. "Still happy you're okay though."

Weston scratches the peach fuzz on his chin. "Skylark is a cool last name. I forgot to mention that earlier," he mutters, as he walks away.

"Thanks." *I've heard that all my life.*

Olivia points to the SUV that they left in earlier. "By the way, the car is over there."

Weston stops in his tracks and looks back at me. "And another thing, where's Marianne?"

I sigh. With all the commotion, I forgot to give them an update on Marianne. "She stayed behind. I'll explain why later."

Weston looks puzzled for a moment, then heads over to the car. "Alright then."

Olivia turns her attention to me. "Well, on a better note, the courthouse seems safe! They have a few officers there, and they check to make sure no one got bit by the zombie things before they let anyone in. I think we should stay there, but what do you think?" Her face lights up.

"Sure. If the place seems safe, we should stay until we come up with a better plan," I respond.

"Okay, let's go!" Olivia walks back over to the SUV. "Oh, and I almost forgot! We found Reese nearby." She points at Reese; he's leaning over the side of the car.

My eyes widen. *I thought he was dead.* "Reese? You're alive?"

His eyes meet with mine and he makes his way over to us. "Yeah, why wouldn't I be?"

My voice elevates a bit. "I woke up and you were nowhere in sight! I assumed you were thrown from the car or something!"

Olivia watches in suspense. "Thrown from the car?"

I totally forgot Oli's listening. "It's not as bad as it sounds."

Reese clenches his fists. "Zombies were coming toward the truck! If I stayed, they were gonna kill us both! We had a better chance separating, so I knocked two bricks together, and I did a lot of yelling to draw them away from the truck."

I feel relief. "Thanks! I'm glad you're alright."

167

Reese walks over to the car and leans his back on it. "Well, I'd like to tag along with you guys, if that's alright?"

Olivia opens the front door. "Sure, as long as you drive."

Reese smiles in satisfaction as he hops in the car.

I pull Olivia to the side. "How's Rob?"

She rubs her hand on her forehead. "He's... I'm not sure. He's been coughing a lot, and he looks really sick...So, I'm guessing he's not doing too well."

Rob is a good guy; he doesn't deserve this. *I guess no one really does.*

Reese downs the window. "Axel, remember

when I told you that zombies are attracted to sound?"

I nod my head as Olivia raises her eyebrow in curiosity.

Reese continues. "Well, Weston shot the zombie, so who knows how many zombies are going to come!"

"Well, what are we waiting for? Let's get going..." Olivia's voice trails off as we see a group of zombies running towards us.

"Time to go!" I hop in the third row and Olivia sits next to me.

Reese puts the gear in drive and presses his foot on the gas. "Is it alright if I head over to a treehouse? I'd like to collect some of my supplies that I left there."

"Sure, whatever gets us away from those things!" Jeffrey shouts from the middle row.

Chapter 20:

<u>The Treehouse</u>

"So, you chose to stay in a treehouse?" I look at Reese in confusion as I'm sitting on the hard wooden floor.

Reese opens a cabinet and pulls out chocolate granola bars. "Yeah. Zombies can't climb ladders...I don't think. Safest area to be in, I suppose." He hands the granola bars to us.

"Now you're talking my language. Thank you!" Olivia chows it down as fast as her mouth will let her.

"Yeah, thank you! I'm so hungry!" I stuff the granola bar in my mouth.

Everyone starts eating, everyone except for Rob. He staggers to his feet and walks to the other end of the treehouse.

Weston glances at Rob, then at me. "So, how come Marianne couldn't come?" he asks while licking the granola residue off the wrapper.

I set my granola wrapper on the floor. "She found her family, so she stayed with them."

"Dang, I'm gonna miss her," Weston reluctantly admits. "She kinda grew on me."

"Only took a few years for her to grow on you," Willow jokes, "but I'm gonna miss her, too…"

Jeremy puts his arm around Willow. "We all will."

We stay quiet for a moment and think about everything we've been through.

Jeffrey breaks the silence. "On a lighter note, I still can't believe we made it out of those situations alive!"

"I know right! We came across zombies and men with guns!" Jeremy beams. "We're unstoppable!"

I stay quiet. Rob isn't as lucky as us. He got bit, because he was selfless and risked his own life for someone he just met. I don't know if I could've done the same thing.

I observe Rob from afar. He's sitting on the opposite end of the treehouse with his back facing us. I can hear faint whimpers.

"I'm gonna check on Rob." I make my way over to Rob and extend a granola bar to him. "Here. You're probably hungry."

He pushes the bar away. "How long until I turn into one of those things?" he asks in a hopeless tone.

His words leave me speechless. He's just accepting his fate without trying to figure out a solution.

"What if you don't turn? You might—"

Tears pour down his face. "Axel, please stop giving me a hope that's not possible...There's no point in pretending I won't turn, we all know I will. The news already explained that."

I can't imagine what he's going through. *Why is this happening...?*

I fight back tears. "I'm...I'm sorry."

"I had big plans after camp..." he mumbles.

"Y-You did?"

"Yup. I found out I was adopted last year. At first, I was heartbroken that I wasn't my parents' biological son, but I soon got over it when they told me that they were searching for my birth parents." He exhales before continuing. "A

172

week before I went to camp, they told me they found my biological parents, but they wanted to meet with them before I did. So, I went to camp while they met with them. Look where that lead me." He lets out a raspy cough.

I can feel the water slowly filling my eyes. Rob is dying and he's right, there's nothing I can do to change that...

Rob forces a smile. "You have a good heart, Axel. Don't let this world change you. I'll be fine though. You should go back to the others."

But he's not fine.

"I'm not just gonna go with everyone else and pretend you're not bit! I don't know why everyone's acting like you're not dying!"

Rob leans his head on a pillow. "Axel, they were all worried about me earlier, too. I just told them to leave me alone, because I hate seeing others upset, especially when it's about me. So please, just go."

I don't want to, but I'm probably making it more difficult for him to cope with what's going on.

I drag my feet across the wooden floor and take a seat beside Olivia.

Olivia looks at me as I sit down and whispers, "You, okay?"

I slowly nod my head.

She watches Rob in the distance. "We're all hurting. It's okay if you don't want to talk about it."

Reese sits on the floor next to us and sighs. "I've been informed of the difficult situation on our hands. It's devastating that anyone has to go through this, especially kids."

Jeremy lays his head on his brother's shoulder. "Yeah. I can't imagine what he's going through."

"Well, I know we can't fix anything, but we can at least let Rob enjoy the last few hours he has before he turns." Reese pulls out a pack of Uno cards from his back pocket.

Weston scoots by us. "Yeah..."

Willow puts her face to her knees. "Rob's going to turn because of me..."

As she finishes, Rob takes a seat beside her.

"Please don't blame yourself."

Willow looks up at him. "B-But…it was my fault!" She squeezes her fists.

"No, it wasn't. I chose to save you, no one told me to. It was my choice, and I wouldn't change what I did. It wasn't your fault, and it never will be."

Man, he's a nice guy. I feel so bad for him.

Weston cautiously gives Rob a hug. "Thank you, Rob. You saved the only person I have left…I'll never forget you." A tear runs down his face, but he quickly wipes it away.

"Okay, no more sorrow, guys! Let's just play some Uno." Rob smiles again, but this time it's a real one.

Reese nods and starts distributing the Uno cards.

....

It's dark once again. It seems like time is flying by. I'm staring out a window, and from what I can see, the woods look so peaceful. I can't see zombies or hear any ear-piercing screams. It's almost like nothing ever happened. Since Rob is…going to turn soon, we all agreed to just stay here at the treehouse until that happens. There's no point in

175

bringing Rob all the way to the courthouse just for them to turn him away.

We couldn't just leave him alone either…It would be harder for him to face this alone. I still can't wrap my head around all of this. Man, I just hope the government gets this virus under control quickly.

Olivia leans her head on my shoulder and pulls me out of my thoughts. I'm sure she realizes I'm upset. She can usually tell when I am.

"I can't believe this is happening." Her voice cracks, which usually happens when she is (or was) crying.

"Yeah…" I wrap my arms around her and continue to stare out the window.

"We should try calling our parents in the morning. Maybe they'll pick up."

"Yeah, hopefully…" I reply as I close the curtain.

I observe everyone's activity in the treehouse. Jeremy and Jeffrey are reading a book (from where I'm sitting it looks like a survival book), Willow and Weston are talking near the treehouse door, and Reese is reloading his gun.

Reese slides his gun in his holster and grabs a box, setting it on the counter.

"I almost forgot." He opens the box. "There are a few bullets and guns in here. Grab what you kids can. You can't survive out here without the proper weapons."

Olivia looks inside the box. "So, do you think it's gonna take a while for the government to deal with the virus?"

Reese scratches his chin. "Yeah, I do. If the virus is as dangerous as the news said, I highly doubt the government will get it under control anytime soon."

Jeremy reaches his hand in the box and touches a gun. He quickly snatches his hand back as soon as it makes contact. "Are guns really necessary?" he stutters.

Jeffrey puts his hand on his brother's shoulder. "Jer, I don't want to use a gun either, but we have we have to protect ourselves...IF NECESSARY." He stresses as he scratches the back of his head. "Just to be clear though, I don't know how to use a gun."

I join the crowd and pull the pistol (that I found in the truck earlier) out of my back pocket. "I know how to use a gun. I can teach you," I reply.

177

Weston waves his hand in the air as he stands up. "I also know how to use a gun, so I can help." He pulls a Glock 19 (a type of pistol) out of his pocket.

Olivia bites her bottom lip. "I still don't think guns are necessary. Violence isn't the answer," she admits.

Reese reaches into his box and hands her a crossbow. "Some people are against violence and that's okay. But you have to understand the situation that we're living in now. If you don't feel comfortable using a gun, just use this crossbow."

"But—"

"It's either that, or you can play nice with the zombies and get bitten. Your choice. I never said you had to kill the zombies with the bow."

She stares at the crossbow and reluctantly accepts it. "Fine."

Jeremy stares at the revolver in the box. "I still don't agree with you guys, but I suppose you all have a point about the gun thing," he sighs. "I've never used a gun, but I've watched many tutorials online on how to properly use one, just in case."

I nod. "That's good, but experience is still the best teacher."

Reese raises his finger in the air. "I forgot to mention," he starts, "when dealing with zombies, try to aim for the head or the heart. If you shoot it anywhere else, you will need more than one bullet to kill it."

So that's why when I shot the zombie in the arm it didn't kill him.

"How do you know all this?" I wrinkle my forehead.

"From the last few days. I had to learn quick."

"Oh." I hand Reese my gun. "Thanks for the advice. Can I get some bullets?"

He twirls the gun in his hand. "A nine-millimeter is a nice gun to have. I'll lend you some bullets." He puts two bullets in the magazine.

Two bullets? He just said that it takes more than one to kill the zombies if I don't aim for the head or the heart, *so what's the point?*

I stare at the magazine in disbelief. "You're only giving me two bullets? I ask. "If I don't aim for a vital part on the zombie, it will be hard to kill those things."

Reese leans against the wall. "There're three things that people grab when chaos erupts: food, water, and guns. And obviously, guns need bullets, so people grab those too. I grabbed what I could when everything started getting bad."

I slide the gun in my pocket. "I guess that makes sense."

Reese lends Jeffrey and Weston a few bullets as well.

Chapter 21:

<u>Goodbye</u>

Rob wakes up from his short nap and yawns. His face is a lot paler than it was a few hours ago. As the rest of us gather our supplies, tears fall down his face.

"I don't want to turn..." he announces, sounding groggy.

Reese keeps his hand on his gun. "I know you don't kid, but there's nothing we can do."

Rob thinks for a moment before continuing. "Yes t-there is..." He points to the gun in Reese's holster.

Reese looks down at his gun, then back at Rob. "Look, I can kill zombies and crazy men, but—"

"Rob, we're not doing that!" Willow angrily shouts while clenching her fists.

"Please...I'd hate to become one of those things..." He lets out a wet cough as he's about to finish his thought. He's looking worse as the minutes go by.

Weston punches the treehouse door, making a slight hole in the wood. "Rob...You sacrificed yourself for my sister, and now you want us to...I need some air!" He opens the door and slams it shut.

Jeffrey puts his hand on Rob's shoulder. "You are one special guy, Rob. We'll never forget you..." He inhales deeply, trying to contain his emotions.

Rob gives a weak smile. "I'll never forget you guys either."

Willow stares at Rob and tears pour down her face. "I'm so sorry!" and she begins to cry.

Rob reaches in his pocket and gives her a mini comic book. "I want you to have this. Don't blame yourself for what happened. I want you to look at this comic and remember that I told you otherwise."

Willow squeezes the comic book in her hand.

Jeremy looks at Rob. "You don't deserve this!" And with that, he walks out of the treehouse, and Jeffrey follows behind him.

Olivia's eyes start to water. "I don't know what hurts worse: that I'm never going to see you again, or that I didn't cherish the moments I had with you more…" She reaches out for a hug, but Rob pushes her away.

"I don't know when I'll turn…but I think it might be any minute now…AHHH!" He lays flat on the ground and rolls from side to side in pain. "Please don't let me turn!"

"ROB? ROB!" I shout.

WHAT'S HAPPENING?

Reese pushes Olivia, Willow, and I out of the treehouse and slams the door shut.

Willow stares at the door in shock. "D-Do you think Rob turned yet?"

I give Willow a hug. "I'm not sure, but hopefully he'll be alright."

POW!
POW!
POW!

The noise came from inside the treehouse. We all stare at each other for a split second before realizing what just happened. *Rob is…he's…gone.* Rob was so positive, so kind, so selfless…I've never experienced loss before. Knowing

183

that someone you care about is gone forever. All Rob wanted was to meet his birth parents...nothing more...

I bang my fists on the treehouse, unable to cope with what's happening. Willow's next to me, mumbling something under her breath with tears dripping down her cheek.

Olivia hugs her knees to her chest. "Axel...he's gone...He's really gone..."

"I know..."

Jeremy, Weston, and Jeffrey are down the ladder talking to each other. I'm sure they heard the gunshots too, so they probably know that Rob...died.

Reese cracks the door open.

"Is he dead? Did he turn?" Willow looks up at Reese.

Do I really want to know?

"I don't know. He took the gun from me, and he shot one of the windows out. Then Rob jumped out...I guess he changed his mind. I don't blame him; I'd rather turn than give up. You never know, there might be a cure one day." Reese stares at the floor as he speaks.

Everyone is frozen with disbelief. We don't know if we should be happy that Rob is still alive or sad that he's gonna turn into one of those things.

Olivia breaks the silence. "We should go! Zombies probably heard the gunshots anyway."

I know this is really affecting her. She just changed the subject.

Reese shrugs his shoulders. "It doesn't matter. They can't climb. Once they realize they can't reach us, they'll go on their way."

Willow brushes past Olivia and looks Reese dead in the eye. "So, you didn't see him turn?" She asks in a soft tone.

"No, but he probably already turned. He's probably not around here though, he was going pretty fast. So, you won't have to worry about seeing him like that."

Good.

In hopes of changing the subject, Reese glances at the sky for a moment. "Since it's dark, we might as well get some sleep before we head out. It's dangerous to travel at night."

"Whatever," Olivia huffs as she swings the treehouse door open.

....

The treehouse is quiet. No one's saying a word. We're all still in shock about what happened today…But I'd rather not think about it.

As we're sitting in silence, Olivia chews on another granola bar.

I didn't realize Reese had any extras.

"After we go to the courthouse, what then? Our parents are probably worried sick about us," she whispers.

That's the first thing Olivia's said in hours.

I lay my head on the cold wooden floor. "I'm not sure. Once we call our parents, we'll probably figure something out."

She tosses the wrapper behind her. "Sounds like a plan."

So much has happened in such little time. And to think, if I just listened to my mom, Olivia and I wouldn't be experiencing any of this. I guess the saying is true, *Mother does know best.*

Olivia glances at me and rubs her chin. "Are you alright? You seem stressed."

Of course I'm stressed! Rob is gone!

I clear my throat. "I'm fine."

"Look Axe, you don't have to pretend like you aren't scared that this is happening. I'm scared too! I'm afraid that Rob won't be the only one of us to turn! I feel like everyone's going to eventually get bit. One after the other and if you turn...I don't know what I'd do!"

She takes a small, shaky breath. "You're one of the closest people to me! I try to act like I'm ok, pretend like I've got everything under control and that I'm some tough kid, but you know how I am. I'm SCARED! So scared..."

"Oli, it's okay—"

She cuts me off. "I feel like those zombies out there are still people. Imagine how their life was like before all of this. Imagine their families and the amazing experiences they had. I'm telling you all of this just to show you that everyone is scared. It's best to let it all out before you end up

187

losing your mind by keeping it all bottled up…" She lays down with her back facing me and all I can hear is her whimpering.

I want to tell her, '*There, there,*' or '*I'm here for you,*' or '*I understand,*' but I know she just needs time by herself. So, I turn on my side and close my eyes.

Chapter 22:

<u>Decisions</u>

SMACK!

My face stings from a slap to my cheek and I instantly open my eyes.

"WAKE UP, AXEL!" Reese grabs my arm and drags me across the wooden floor.

I pull my arm from Reese's grip and hastily get off the dirty floor. "I'm awake! I'm awake!" I rub my arm. "Why were you dragging me?"

Jeremy points behind me. "Because a zombie's in the treehouse!"

I look behind me and somehow a zombie made his way up the ladder and into the treehouse!

The zombie reaches his arms out and tries to grab me!

"Axel, WATCH OUT!" Olivia yells.

I quickly dodge out of the zombie's way, but I slip and hit my head on the ground and slowly lose consciousness.

....

"You ok Axel?" I hear Olivia's faint voice as I slowly wake up.

I look around the cabin. I don't see the zombie anywhere. "Yeah...Where's the zombie?"

Olivia sighs. "Reese took care of it, I guess those things can climb...which makes this situation a thousand times better," she replies sarcastically.

Reese hands me a bookbag. "You can keep your things in here but just keep your gun on you at all times."

I put the bag on. "Thanks."

"Guys! I see zombies in the distance! We should get moving!" Jeffrey shouts from outside the treehouse.

Jeremy moves the curtain back and looks outside the window to get a better view of the zombies. He then starts counting on his hands. "Yeah, based on my calculations, if we stay here much longer, those things will catch up to us in no time."

"Then let's go!" Jeffrey slides down the ladder.

"Come on, Willow." Weston holds her hand and follows behind Jeffrey.

"I can walk on my own." Willow snatches her hand from his grip.

Weston mumbles something under his breath as he follows behind her.

....

We arrive at the county government complex, and a few officers stand guard in front of the buildings.

"There's a parking spot." Reese parks the SUV and turns it off. "Let's go."

I get out of the SUV and quicken my pace toward the courthouse. "I hope this place is as safe as it looks," I utter as I observe the police.

Olivia puts her arm around my shoulder. "Axel, you're always skeptical about something."

I raise my eyebrow. "Since when have I been skeptical? I'm just being careful."

She lowers her tone. "Trust me, this place IS as safe as it looks. Just let us do the talking since we were here yesterday."

As we approach the building, a man with a black suit is standing next to three officers guarding the entrance.

Olivia extends her hand. "Hi Mister Mayor!"

He shakes Oli's hand. "Hi again, young lady. Glad to see you made it back in one piece," he responds while fixing his tie. "As you already know, we have to make sure there are no bites on any of you."

A few more officers come out of the building. They lift our sleeves and pat us down.

"I don't see anything, sir," an officer says, as the others walk back inside the courthouse.

The mayor sighs with satisfaction. "Alright, well, you all can head inside the courthouse. That's where the other citizens are." He pulls a few packs of crackers out of his pocket. "Here are crackers for you all." He distributes the crackers and walks in a different direction; two officers follow him.

Weston holds the courthouse door open. "Let's go."

We pass through the security metal detectors (not that any officers were checking us).

"It's weird that officers aren't by the security area," Willow whispers.

Jeffrey shrugs his shoulders. "I guess they don't need to frisk anyone during an apocalypse."

A crowd forms ahead of us, going in one direction.

"Why is everyone walking in the same direction?" Jeffrey wonders as he observes the crowd.

Weston points ahead. "Someone's directing the traffic."

I look ahead and see a short, chubby man standing beside the elevator, pointing his hands frantically.

"THIS WAY! OVER HERE!" The man yells, waving his hands to the left.

Reese follows the crowd. "Hm. Let's go that way then."

Olivia grips my arm. "I don't want to get lost in the crowd." She locks her arm with mine as we continue to walk through the building.

"Don't worry, you won't," I reply, moving my arm from her grip and placing it around her shoulder.

A tall man wearing a white suit is holding a door open that leads to a courtroom.

"This way, come on!" he shouts.

We enter the courtroom and sit down near the front of the court. There's a man and two girls sitting a row in front of us, with an elderly woman beside them. More people come inside the room and sit down.

"There's a lot of people in here," Jeffrey observes as he watches more people enter.

A few more families walk inside until all the seats are filled.

BOOM!
The door shuts.

I hear a lot of commotion outside the doors.

"HEAD TO THE NEXT COURTROOM! THERE IS NO MORE SPACE IN THERE!" A man outside the door shouts.

There must be a lot of people out there.

The man that's sitting in the row in front of us (with the two girls) stands up and slams his fists on the seat.

"SOMEBODY TELL US WHAT'S GOING ON!"

Another man, around the age of fifty, takes a seat at the judge's bench, accompanied by an officer.

A young woman stands up from her seat behind us. "Why are people eating people?"

The man at the judge's bench raises both his hands in the air, signaling everyone to calm down. "Settle down, please! My name is Russell Conn, and I am the city manager. I will tell you all what's going on." He clears his throat and lets out a smoker's cough.

"THEN TELL US ALREADY!" Weston yells, standing up from his seat.

Willow looks up at her brother in disappointment. "Really, Weston?" she whispers.

Weston's cheeks turn red due to embarrassment. "Well, we have the right to know."

Russell Conn fixes his tie. "There has been a virus outbreak...We lied to the public, telling everyone that it did not exist. We assumed that we would be able to take care of the matter before things got worse. Obviously, that didn't happen—"

"How did it come about?" Reese inquires, listening eagerly.

Russell wipes the sweat dripping down his forehead. "I don't have that information at this time. We assume that it might've originated from another country, or an animal. Some even believe this disease was made in a laboratory."

"Then what are you sure of?" The young woman behind me asks.

"If someone gets bitten by one of those things, they turn into one within a couple of hours. Unless they are killed before they turn," Russell replies with a sigh.

A woman in a pantsuit raises her hand. "I also heard that it may be a mutation of the rabies virus. Can you verify this information?"

Russell stretches his collar. "The CDC is yet to confirm that theory."

Jeffrey stands up from his chair. "Or is that another thing you're keeping from the public?"

Russell lowers his head. "That is all I know."

Olivia raises her hand. "Why did the news tell us to come here?"

"Until the National Guard arrives, we want the citizens to be safe. This building is large and sturdy, so it will do for now. There are also a few officers here, so hopefully they can help if those monsters get in," Russell finishes.

"How long do you think it will be until the National Guard comes?" I ask, curious.

"Who knows. I'm sure the larger cities are very hectic, so this probably isn't the first place they'd protect. But we can assure you that the situation is under control." He stands up from the bench and heads to the door.

"Wait! Is it global?" An older woman asks.

"We don't think so, but we're not getting much information at this time," he responds while opening the door.

The officer follows behind Russell. "Food will be brought to you all, so stay here until then."

The door shuts behind them.

Olivia leans back in the seat beside me. "When we came here earlier, it was less organized. That's why it took us so long. We also had to take a lot of back roads to get here, and we kept getting lost," she whispers.

"Because of zombies?"

She nods. "Yup, and crazy people."

My phone starts ringing in my pocket and people start staring in my direction. I pull my phone out, and the caller ID is Mom! *The calls are finally going through!* I dash to a quiet corner in the room and answer the call.

"M-Mom?" I nervously ask, hoping it's not too good to be true.

"AXEL!? My baby's okay!" she shouts.

I hold back tears as I hear her voice. "Hey Mom. It's good to hear your voice!"

"You too...I've been trying to call you for days, but the calls wouldn't go through."

"Yeah, the same thing was happening to me and Olivia."

I hear her gasp on the phone.

"Olivia's with you! Oh, thank goodness! I was hoping you two were still together."

I chuckle. "Yeah, we listened to you. Stuck together like glue," I reply as I glance at Olivia. "Gosh, it's good to hear from you, Mom."

"Yeah. Look, I'm heading to Georgia. They won't allow people to fly since that outbreak is spreading, but I have to figure something out."

My eyes widen. "No mom! Please don't come here! Those zombies are crawling all over this town. It will keep getting worse the longer I wait for you here!"

"Zombies?"

"Yeah—They act like zombies, so that's what I call them."

"Oh." She remains silent for a few seconds. "Well, I can't just stay here and do nothing, Axel! I have to get to you!"

I fall silent. I don't want her putting herself, August, or Hayden in danger. But I can't travel all the way to California to them either. That's way too far, especially when I have to avoid crazy people and monsters. But maybe there's somewhere we can travel that's not too far away.

Mom sniffs. "Axel? Y-You still there?"

"Mom, what if we head to your cabin in Michigan?"

"Um..."

199

I can hear her biting her nails through the phone.

I open my mouth to speak before she has time to rebuttal. "It's safer to head to Michigan than for me to stay and wait for you here."

She mumbles something under her breath. "F-Fine…But promise me one thing! You will call me every night! I want to know you're okay!"

"I promise Mom."

"Okay, but—" Her voice cuts off mid-sentence.

I stare at my phone and realize the call disconnected. "Dang it!" I redial her number, but the signal is busy.

Oli, overhearing my conversation, walks over to me. "I guess the signal went out…"

I smack my hand on my forehead in frustration. "Yeah—I guess so."

"I heard you on the phone with your mom…I'm happy you got to talk to her," she smiles, trying to hide her sorrow.

"I wish your mom called you."

"She probably did, but I accidentally left my phone back at the treehouse, so I'll never know. Hopefully we get a good signal soon, so I can call her from your phone."

Out of nowhere, the lights start flickering on and off.

"Don't tell me the lights are about to go out," Olivia mutters.

And to her horror, the lights shut off completely. If it wasn't for the tiny bit of light shining from a window, I wouldn't be able to see my hand in front of my face.

Chapter 23:

<u>The Power's Out</u>

"WHAT'S GOING ON?" A female voice shouts.

"WHY DID THE LIGHTS TURN OFF?" Another adds.

I guess they're all pretty freaked out too. But it's hard to make out any faces in the darkness (like I said, the window is only shining a tiny bit of light inside).

I hear the door push open.

"EVERYONE CALM DOWN!" A male voice exclaims. "It's me, Russell. The power went out, but don't panic."

"What do you mean the power went out, Russell?" Reese asks (I can't see him, but I can hear his voice).

"It's not working! I guess a fuse blew or something, but it's not like anyone's at the power company to fix the issue!" Russell shouts, his voice a bit raspy.

"So, what do we do?" Jeffrey's voice echoes in the room.

"An officer knows where a few flashlights are, so we'll have to rely on them to see in the dark. At least, until I figure something else out. It won't be the best thing, but it'll have to do," Russell explains.

The door slams shut. I sit in the dark for a few more minutes before I hear the door open again. An officer turns a flashlight on and holds a few others in his hands.

"Finally!" I hold my hand in front of my eyes.

The officer projects his voice. "I only have four, so can everyone line up in an orderly fashion—"

People start racing to him, trying to get their hands on a flashlight.

Oli and I just stay where we are. There's no point in trying to grab one. *It's very unlikely that we'd get anything.*

Jeremy approaches us while pointing a bright light in my face. "I got a flashlight!"

I push the flashlight out of my face. "How?" I stare in shock.

Jeremy smirks. "Easy. Before he finished, I just calculated the amount of people that were in the room, then added how many steps I would need to take to reach him, and—"

"Actually, I'd rather not know," I laugh.

The rest of our group head over to us.

"Nice job, Jer!" Jeffrey beams with satisfaction.

"Too bad there's only one window in here. It's still kinda dark even with the flashlight," Weston notes.

Willow leans her head on Weston's shoulder. "Yeah, that's true."

Olivia glares at Weston, then tugs on my sleeve. "Can we talk for a second?"

"Uh, can it wait?" I whisper.

"No. Come on." She pulls my arm, and I reluctantly follow her.

We stand in a dimly lit corner of the courtroom, and she stares at Weston once again before telling me what's going on. "I don't trust Weston."

Those are words I never thought I'd hear anyone in the group say.

"Why? Weston is a good friend to us, he's loyal and—"

She grits her teeth. "No, he's not."

"Are you gonna elaborate?" I snap.

She lets out an annoyed huff before continuing. "Rob is dead."

I lean my hand on the wall. "Yeah, I'm aware."

Olivia places both her hands on my shoulders (which was hard to do since she's short). "Axel, just listen. Rob got bit because he saved Willow from the zombie that was in the basement."

"Yeah, we already know this," I groan, not wanting to relive the horror.

She plasters a worried look on her face. "But Weston and Willow told us that there were no zombies down there, remember?"

Wait...*Oli is right.* They told us that there was nothing in the basement. Why would they lie to us? Rob would have been alive if they just told us the truth.

"I'll be back." I brush past Olivia and make my way over to Weston. He's standing beside Jeremy and Willow, laughing about something.

"Weston, we need to talk," I whisper, only loud enough for him to hear.

Weston raises his eyebrow. "What's this about?"

"Trust me, you don't want everyone involved. Just follow me."

He wrinkles his forehead and reluctantly follows behind. "Alright then."

I take him to the same corner Oli and I were standing at just a moment ago.

"Oli, give us a second, alright?"

"Fine," she walks back over to everyone else.

Weston rubs his arm with his hand. "Are you going to tell me what the heck is going on?"

I clench my fists in anger. "You lied to us, Weston! Rob turned, because you knew there was a zombie in your basement, and you didn't tell us!"

His eyes widen in surprise. "It wasn't my fault…" He sits down on the ground.

"What do you mean it wasn't your fault? You knew there was a zombie in your basement, didn't you?" I sit down beside him with fury in my eyes.

"That zombie was my mom!" A tear runs down his face, but he quickly wipes it away. "Willow was going to tell you guys, but I told her not to. I thought you guys would just try to kill my mom, but I guess that's what happened any-way...I'm so stupid." He hits his hand on his head.

Weston never shares his feelings or shows any sign of weakness, so it's weird seeing him like this. I can't im-agine what he's going through. It's bad enough that his mom turned into a zombie, but Rob too...

Weston twiddles his thumbs. "My mom was always trying to make ends meet," he sighs, reminiscing on his past. "My dad left when I was around ten, so she had to raise us on her own."

"That must've been hard," I reply, thinking about my own dad.

"Yeah, it was. I always thought it was my duty to pr-otect my mom and Willow since he left. I had to be the man of the house, look after them, but it got annoying after a while. That's why I went to camp. I needed a break from all my responsibilities: working and babysitting. But if I never went to camp maybe I could've saved my mom, and Rob wouldn't be gone..."

I stand up. "Anyone can say that they could've or should've done something, but it's not your fault. It's not like you knew this was gonna happen."

207

He nods his head in agreement.

"But I know what you mean. I feel the same way. I'm from California and my mom—"

He interrupts. "Gosh! From all the way over there? Why did you travel so far for Camp Lovely?"

I scratch the back of my neck in embarrassment. "My mom signed Olivia and I up for the wrong camp."

"Yikes."

"I know, right?"

Weston stands up and dusts the dirt off his jeans. "Well, is that all you wanted to talk about?"

I was going to talk about my past, but it's probably better to keep it to myself.

"Yeah, pretty much." I get off the ground and head over to the rest of the group.

"Thanks for asking me what happened before bringing it up to everyone else," he whispers as we're walking.

"No problem."

When I first met Weston, I assumed that he was just a self-centered jock, but now that I know him more, I realize there's always more than meets the eye. He's had a difficult life, and it's not like this virus is making it any better for him.

Chapter 24:

Plan Backfires

Oli and I are sitting on a bench near a corner in the courtroom. We've been planning all day for our long trip to Michigan, and we'll probably head out once morning arrives. *I'm gonna miss everyone, but who knows, maybe someone will want to tag along with us.*

Olivia searches through her bag. "I'm glad we have a plan now," she whispers.

"Yeah." I sneak a peek into her bag. "Anything good to eat in there? I'm starving."

She closes her bag. "Nope. Not even a crumb..." She holds her stomach. "I think I left the beef jerky pack at the camp."

"It's fine. I'm sure we'll find something to eat soon—" My thoughts are interrupted when I notice a zombie trying to breach the entrance of the courthouse.

POP!

POP!

POP!

A cop shoots the zombie, and it crashes to the ground.

That was lucky.

Some people in the room jump at the sound of the gunshots.

I watch as Reese jerks his head toward the window and squints hard. "Great. More are on their way," he huffs as he gathers his belongings.

Jeremy watches Reese pack his bag. "Where are you going?"

"Leaving. There's no point in staying." He zips his bag up and walks toward the exit.

Jeffrey stands in his way. "But it's not like they could get in, right? It's safe here…"

Weston stands in front of the door and chimes in. "Yeah, can we stop running for one second? If zombies try to get in, we'll just escape before they attack any of us."

Reese slides his bookbag on his shoulders. "They're attracted to noise. Who knows how many zombies will head over here!"

211

Jeremy places his arm on Reese's shoulder. "Well then, we'll come with you! Just give us a few minutes to pack our things."

Weston rolls his eyes at Jeremy's response. "Whatever."

Reese rubs his chin. "Fine, just make it quick."

Olivia stands up and slides her bag on. "I'm gonna join the others."

"Same here." I follow closely behind her, and we join the rest of the group.

Jeremy puts a few things in his bag. "I have a question. Should we have a leader? You know, in case we don't agree on something?"

Weston holds his stomach and lets out a quiet chuckle. "Why would I need anyone to lead me? I can take care of myself and my sister," he grunts while showing off his biceps.

Olivia wrinkles her forehead. "Well, if you were paying attention, you would have heard that we should have a leader to make the final decision!"

I don't even know why Olivia's getting involved. We're not even staying with them.

Weston, taken back by her response, leans close to Olivia. "What's your problem?"

Olivia stomps her foot on the ground, not backing down for one second. "Maybe Axel believes that little excuse you had about that zombie in your basement, but I don't buy it for one second!" She looks him straight in the eyes.

She heard that?

Weston doesn't look fazed by her remark at all. I believe him, but if I know one thing about Olivia, it's that she can spread rumors like wildfire. So, if he doesn't want this story getting out, he should clear things up with her.

Willow opens her mouth to say something, but Weston covers her mouth and shakes his head. "You're not worth our time."

Olivia grunts and stands beside me.

"Not sure what that's about," Jeremy sighs. "But who wants to be leader?"

Olivia raises her hand. "Me!"

"Sh! There are other people in here, ya know!" An older man grunts as he walks past us.

Olivia rubs the back of her head in embarrassment. "Like I was saying—"

"Can't we talk about this leader stuff some other time? We should just get out of here first," I interrupt.

Reese nods. "Yeah, Axel's right. We can deal with this later."

Olivia twirls a strand of hair around her finger. "Fine."

POP!

POP!

POP!

Reese turns around. "You guys heard that, right?"

I nod my head nervously. "Yeah."

Willow tugs on her brother's sleeve. "Were those gunshots?"

"Sounded like it," Weston gulps.

I glance out the window from a distance.

If something is out there, I don't want to be near the window to find out.

Before I can get a clear look, the window shatters and zombies start pouring into the courtroom! Time seems to slow down, and I watch in horror as the flesh-eating monsters devour everyone in their path. I see Weston swing Willow on his back and race for the door.

As he runs past me, he tugs on my sleeve. "AXEL, RUN!"

I snap out of it and run for the door, following the crowd of terrified people. As I'm almost at the court room door, I hear a familiar voice screaming behind me.

"AHH!"

I turn my head around and Olivia is cornered by two zombies!

Oh no...

The zombies are dragging their feet while reaching their arms out wide, trying to grab her! She swings a baseball bat back and forth in hopes of stopping the zombies from getting any closer, but it doesn't seem to be working.

"HELP!!" She cries.

I hear another familiar shriek to my left. In a split second, I turn, and to my horror, Jeffrey is surrounded by five zombies.

Our eyes meet and his eyes light up in relief.

"Axel!" he yells, staring hopelessly.

I want to help Jeffrey, but Olivia's in danger too. I can't just leave her...I promised our parents that I'd look out for her.

There's no time to think. *I need to get Olivia out of here fast, so I'll have time to save Jeffrey.* "Maybe there's something I can use to help Olivia," I mumble.

I dig my hand in my pocket and feel my gun.

I completely forgot about it!

I point my gun at one of the zombies that's surrounding Olivia and pull the trigger.

POP!

The zombie crashes to the ground with a BANG, but I know that will only last for a moment. *They don't just die by one gunshot if you don't shoot them in the head or the heart.*

"Come on, Oli!" I grab her arm and pull her to the exit.

I skim the room for Jeffrey, but he's nowhere to be found. The zombies that were once surrounding him are now feeding on something nearby.

216

I hope that's not him.

It can't be him.

I rush out of the door with Olivia not far behind, not wanting to know the truth.

Chapter 25:

<u>The Woods</u>

Now that we're deep enough in the woods, me and Olivia stop running and catch our breaths.

Olivia rests her hands on her knees. "I can't believe that just happened." She sits on the soft grass.

I sit down beside her.

Hopefully we're finally safe from the zombies.

"Why did all of those zombies flood the courtroom like that?" Olivia coughs a little.

I take a deep breath. "Maybe whoever shot the gun was close to the window."

"Maybe." She pushes her wild curls out of her face. "You didn't have to save me, you know. I can handle myself."

I shake my head. "Because of me, you don't have to walk around as a mindless zombie. So, you're welcome."

Olivia can't just set aside her pride for one second to thank me for rescuing her.

Olivia stares at me, almost like she's reading my thoughts. "Yeah, I guess you're right, so thanks."

"Now, was that so hard?" I chuckle as I place my arm around her.

She playfully pushes me. "Oh, shush!"

I lay down on the tall, green grass and admire the calming atmosphere. There was so much chaos at that courthouse, so I don't mind the peace and quiet out here in the woods.

Olivia rests her head beside mine. "Well, what now?"

What now? I ponder the question. We could wait here and hope that the others make their way back to us, or we could head back to the treehouse that Reese let us stay in. *I think that's the better option.*

"We could head back to the treehouse. Hopefully the others will head there too, if they made it out..." I trail off and start thinking about Jeffrey.

"Sounds like a plan." She stands up and trudges through the thick woods toward the treehouse.

I follow closely behind her as the image of Jeffrey screaming my name flashes through my mind. If she knew

219

what happened to Jeffrey…What I did…I highly doubt she'd ever talk to me again.

And I wouldn't blame her.

....

As we approach the treehouse, I hear a few zombies nearby, but I can't see them anywhere.

"Look!" Olivia points at the treehouse, and I spot a few zombies walking along the perimeter.

"Well, that's definitely off limits," I mutter.

Olivia stomps her foot. "Great. Those creeps aren't leaving anytime soon."

I rub my hand on my chin. "We should move further into the woods. We don't want those zombies seeing us."

"I agree."

We head in the opposite direction of the treehouse and wander for about ten minutes, until the treehouse is barely in sight.

I notice a few logs lying on the ground nearby.

220

"We're probably going to need a fire for tonight, so I think we could use these," I explain, while pointing at the logs.

"Yeah, you're right! Do you know how to make a fire?" She tilts her head in curiosity.

I look down at the wood and ponder on the question. "I know the basics, I guess."

....

"All we have is wood. We can't spark a fire with just wood, Olivia. I've already tried a million times." I toss a log on the ground.

Olivia puts her hands on her hips. "Axel, if you'd just let me do it, I could actually make a fire."

As I'm getting ready to rebuttal, I hear twigs snapping on the ground, and I immediately turn around. But to my surprise, it's not an animal or a zombie…It's Jeremy!

Jeremy slowly approaches us and leans his back on a nearby tree. "Hey guys!"

221

"Jeremy!" I give him a pat on the back. "I'm glad you're alright!"

Olivia gives him a hug. "Me too."

Jeremy starts breathing heavily as he looks around. "Is J-Jeffrey with you guys-s?"

My blood runs cold for a moment. For a few minutes I forgot Jeffrey's horrifying screams back at the courthouse...But now everything's coming back to me. I can't tell Jeremy what happened. *He'd kill me.* But anyone would have saved the person they're closest to, *right?*

Olivia puts her hand on his shoulder. "He's not with us... I was hoping he was with you!"

Jeremy frantically looks from side to side. "Jeffrey! Where are you?!" he cries.

Olivia forcefully covers his mouth and motions for him to be quiet. "Remember what Reese said? The monsters are attracted by noise!"

A few zombies slowly approach us and try to pinpoint where the sound came from. I immediately duck behind a bush, and Olivia and Jeremy hide next to me.

Olivia rests her hand on Jeremy's shoulder. "I'm sure Jeffrey's fine. He's super athletic AND he's smart. I bet he outran those zombies and is hoping you're safe too," she whispers.

I look at Jeremy. Tears are slowly filling his eyes, and I can't help but wipe a few from my cheek. *I could have saved him, but it would have risked Oli's life...*

As the last zombie walks by, Jeremy brushes past us and runs deeper into the woods.

"Where is he going?" Olivia bolts after him, and I follow behind.

As we make our way through the woods, Jeremy stops where the trees end, and the street begins. He sits on the grass and his hands start shaking.

Olivia stands in front of him. "What are you doing?"

He doesn't respond to Olivia; he just stares at the road ahead of him.

Olivia bends down and looks him in the eye. "Jeremy, your brother is fine!"

"Do you really believe that?" He wipes the sweat off his forehead.

223

"I do. Jeffrey is strong and capable. I know he's alright."

I remain quiet. *I can't lie to him, and I don't want to tell him the truth, either.*

Jeremy's face lights up. "Yeah, you're right! Thanks, Olivia—" He lets out a loud raspy cough, and he immediately squeezes his chest.

"Are you okay?" I ask, as he takes a few breaths.

"Yeah. It's just my asthma. Sadly, I lost my inhaler back at the courthouse, so I need to remain calm until I find another one. I don't want to have an asthma attack when my inhaler is nowhere in sight."

"So, we need to get you an inhaler!" Olivia replies.

"Yeah." He takes his glasses off his head and extends them to me. "I heard you guys struggling with the fire earlier. My glasses could help us make one!"

With guilt, I grab his glasses. "Thanks."

"And one more thing!" He points near a pile of rocks. "I think I saw tinder and flint over there!"

"Okay." I walk over there while Olivia stays with him.

I can't bear to see the hope in his eyes, especially since I know Jeffrey won't be coming back.

I find the flint (I used to watch a survival show, and it taught me a few things), and as I'm reaching for it, I hear a crackling sound nearby. I crouch down and spot a deer munching on the grass.

"Wow...a deer..." I slowly reach for my gun and aim at it.

Olivia tiptoes toward me and lowers my gun. "Don't shoot! It's too loud. Use this instead." She hands me a crossbow and says, "Reese was right. This bow is handy."

I hand the crossbow back to her. "I don't know how to use this, so it's probably best if you shoot."

"I haven't been able to hurt a zombie, much less a deer," she frowns.

"Oli! We don't know when we'll be able to look for food so—"

"Okay, okay!" She grabs the weapon from my hand and aims the crossbow at the deer's head, closes her eyes, and shoots.

Chapter 26:

<u>The Fire</u>

I watch the sun as it slowly sets. The sky becomes a reddish orange, and a little bit of sunlight remains.

"There's not much sunlight left," I mumble.

Jeremy pours a drop of water into the lens of his glasses. He then angles the lens toward the sun and focuses the beam of light into one small area. After a couple of seconds, a small fire erupts.

Olivia smiles in satisfaction. "Nice job Jeremy!"

"Yeah, good job!" I watch as the fire gets bigger.

He rubs his hands above the fire to get warm. "Thanks. I was a boy scout when I was younger, and they taught me a thing or two about survival."

"Well, I watched survival shows when I was younger, so I know a few things about living on the land, too." I inch closer to the small fire.

"So," Olivia pokes the deer. "This deer is way too big to put on a stick, so how are we going to cook it over the fire?"

Jeremy rubs his chin with his hand. "We could cut it. The only problem is that we have nothing to use that would be strong enough to penetrate it."

Olivia pulls something out of her pocket and tosses a knife on the ground.

She has a knife?

"Found this back at the courthouse! It's called a Fixed Blade Knife or something. It's supposed to be good for cutting animals."

Jeremy picks the knife up and starts cutting the deer. "I kind of know how to clean animals. My boy scout leader explained it to me once."

Once he cleans the deer (to the best of his ability), I place a few pieces on a long stick over the fire and watch it slowly cook.

Olivia leans her head on my shoulder. "We should head to a pharmacy in the morning, so Jeremy can get an inhaler."

Jeremy wipes his glasses. "Sounds like a plan."

My heart stings every time I see him happy.

"It's settled then. Tomorrow we'll find supplies at a local pharmacy, then go look for our friends," Olivia orders.

"Cool," I mumble.

I wish none of this ever happened. If I had never gone on this stupid camping trip, me and Olivia would've been fine, and Jeffrey wouldn't be dead...*I bet Rob wouldn't be either.*

Chapter 27:

<u>Operation: Pharmacy</u>

I watch the sun slowly rise above the trees. Morning's finally arriving, which means one thing, *we have to leave soon.* I'm sitting beside Olivia, and Jeremy's lying next to her. From the looks of it, Olivia's fast asleep, but I'm not so sure about Jeremy. He's been tossing and turning for hours.

I let them (well, Olivia) get a few more minutes of sleep before I wake them up, which doesn't bother me, because I can admire the scenery for a little while longer.

Jeremy sits up once he realizes I'm awake.

"Morning," I say as I eat a small piece of deer.

That tastes disgusting.

"Hey." He stretches his arms and lets out a loud yawn. "Do you miss your parents? Well, I guess that's a dumb question."

I brush the dirt off my shoes. "Yeah, of course I do."

"I want to look for my parents once I find Jeffrey. I want to make sure they're okay."

I clench my fists. *I owe it to Jeremy to help him look for his parents.*

"We can look for them with you."

His face lights up. "You guys would look for my parents with me?"

"Of course! I remember you guys mentioning that you live here, so it won't be out of our way."

"Thanks Axel, I owe you."

No, I owe you.

"So, where are you and Olivia planning on going?"

"To Michigan," I explain. "Our parents have a cabin up there, and we're planning on meeting them there."

Jeremy's taken aback. "Wow, that's far! I wish you guys the best of luck."

"You and me both."

He gets off the ground and stares at the woods. "I'm going to see if I can find any more water around here. I don't

230

have any left." Jeremy grabs a stick off the ground and quietly heads deeper into the woods.

Not sure how a stick is supposed to help him.

I reach for my bag, but it's not near the "campsite". I must've left it back at the courthouse.

Great.

Olivia slowly opens her eyes and eases beside me. "I had the weirdest dream about school."

"That's random."

She laughs. "I know, right? We haven't been to school since the beginning of June...It's still July, right?"

"I think so. Blame Counselor James for not letting us look at the calendar on our phones," I laugh a little, then sigh.

"Are you okay, Axe? You seem bothered by something."

I think for a moment before answering. I could tell Olivia what happened to Jeffrey, but if Jeremy somehow overhears, he'll never forgive me. Plus, I don't really want Olivia knowing right now.

"It doesn't matter, I'm fine..." I stare off into the distance and watch Jeremy search for water.

231

She turns my head toward her. "If something's up, you can tell me, Axel."

"I know, but trust me, I'm fine."

She remains quiet for a second. "You didn't get bit, right?" Her voice cracks a little.

"No! I didn't get bit!"

She grabs her bag. "Well, if you're not gonna tell me, then I won't press any further."

She's definitely gonna ask more questions later.

Jeremy comes back empty handed. "I didn't find any water, but maybe there will be some at the pharmacy."

"Maybe," Olivia sighs.

Jeremy points to the right. "Well, from what I can remember, there should be a pharmacy somewhere around here, so follow me."

I follow Jeremy closely as we make our way through the woods.

"There it is." Jeremy whispers.

The pharmacy is a stand-alone building with a few abandoned cars in its parking lot. The building has a light blue coat, and a few of its windows are broken. I notice a lot of zombies wandering around the parking lot.

"There's a ton of zombies walking around. At least they don't see us," I whisper.

"They haven't seen us *yet*." Olivia backs away slowly. "We should head back."

I try to reassure her. "We can't turn back now, we're already here. Plus, we can avoid those zombies."

Jeremy agrees. "He's right, Olivia."

The more I think about it, the less I believe that we'll get inside unnoticed. "We might need a distraction."

Jeremy raises his index finger. "I have an idea! I could distract them. I used to come here often, so I know my way around the store." He points at the zombies as he continues. "I could lead them toward the other side of the store while you guys get the supplies!"

Olivia taps her finger on her chin. "Yeah, that sounds like a plan."

I feel like I owe it to Jeffrey to look out for his twin brother. I have to make sure nothing happens to him. *It's the only thing that will ease my conscience.*

"I'm not sure if that's a good idea, Jeremy!" I disagree.

Jeremy tries his best to appear brave. "Thanks for worrying, but you don't have to! I've calculated everything!"

"What about your asthma?" I ask, hoping that he'll back out.

Jeremy takes a deep breath. "You guys are going to get the inhaler, so once I'm done running, I'll just use it really fast!"

"I guess you have an answer for everything, huh?" I mutter under my breath.

Jeremy nods his head proudly. "Yup."

Olivia watches as more zombies enter the store. "Alright, Jeremy. Ready to go?"

"It's now or never." He takes off running inside and yells, "COME AND GET ME ZOMBIES!"

Olivia tugs on my sleeve. "Alright, there's our opening. Come on!"

As I reluctantly follow behind her, I mumble, "nothing better happen to him, or I'll never forgive myself."

Olivia stares at me for a moment, then runs inside.

She probably heard what I said.

I run on the snack aisle and grab a bag of chips. "There's still a good bit of supplies here," I whisper as I put the chips in Olivia's bag.

"Yeah." She takes her bag off and places a few snacks inside as well. "I'm happy Jeremy's not thinking about Jeffrey anymore. We're not a hundred percent sure his brother's okay, and I feel bad pretending he is."

I ignore her altogether and continue tossing food in her bag. I didn't mean to ignore her; I just didn't know what to say.

"Fine, ignore me then," she huffs.

I change the subject. "We should probably split up; we'll find more supplies that way. Plus, I might find a bag that I can use."

"Yeah, you're probably right."

Olivia heads to an aisle a few rows down, while I hop over the pharmacy counter and look for medicine.

235

There are a few prescription meds scrambled across the floor. "I need to find an inhaler." I start tossing medicine around in hopes of finding an inhaler somewhere around here.

"Bingo!" I snatch a prescription inhaler from off the ground. "Hopefully this is good enough."

I notice a black drawstring bag laying on the corner of the counter, so I grab it and stuff everything inside (I prefer the bookbag that Reese gave me, but I left it at the courthouse).

As I hop back over the counter, I'm met by an older woman with blonde hair.

The woman steps closer. "Sir? Can you help me?"

A little hesitant, I keep my distance from the strange woman and back up a little. "Uh, how can I help?"

"Do you have food? Anything helps."

Olivia makes her way back to me, and her eyes widen as she notices the woman. "Who is she?"

"I'm not sure. She said she needs help."

Olivia stands between me and the woman. "Sorry Ma'am, but we can't help you. There's still some food here, so just get it yourself." She pulls my arm and heads for the exit.

To my shock, the woman pulls out a gun!

"No! I want your food and medicine NOW!"

I pull my gun out in a flash. I aim it at the woman and clear my throat. "It doesn't have to end like this. Just walk away."

I really hope she drops her weapon. It was already a lot having to shoot those zombies. I can't bear to shoot a normal person!

The woman's hand shakes as she tries to keep her gun steady. "No! Give me your stuff!"

Olivia points her crossbow at the lady. "Ma'am—!"

"PLAN BACKFIRING! RUN!" Jeremy rushes past us and a crowd of zombies follow him.

The older woman watches in horror and takes off running in a different direction.

"You don't have to tell me twice!" I reach for a few items and run as fast as my legs will let me toward the campsite.

Chapter 28:

<u>Next Steps</u>

Me and Olivia arrive at the campsite soon after Jeremy. I could've ran faster, but I wanted to stay with Olivia in case one of the zombies caught up to her.

I stop the moment I see Jeremy gasping for air.

He extends his hand toward me. "I-Inhaler…please…"

I search through my bag and grab the inhaler. "Here you go."

He presses the inhaler a few times before feeling relief.

"You alright, bud?" I ask.

"Yeah…" He sits down on the grass. "The zombies aren't still chasing you guys, are they?" He speaks slowly, so he can catch his breath.

Olivia lays her head on the ground. "Nope. That woman was screaming so much, they lost interest in us and went after her."

"Speaking of which," Jeremy coughs a little, "who was that lady, anyway?"

Olivia huffs at the thought of the woman. "She was crazy! She was going to shoot us over some supplies!"

Jeremy shakes his head in disappointment. "I'm not surprised. If people don't have the things they need to survive, they'll do anything to get it." He takes another puff of his inhaler. "Especially if they have a family."

"I guess that's true," I look over at Jeremy unzipping Olivia's bag.

He pulls a few things out of her bag and stares in awe. "How did you find all these supplies? You found a few snacks and some bandages!"

Olivia beams with pride. "All in a day's work, but I can't take all the credit. Axel tossed a few snacks in my bag, too." She zips her bag closed. "Speaking of which, what did you get Axe?"

I open my bag. "Aside from the inhaler, I got some beef jerky packs and over-the-counter medicine."

"That's so smart! I didn't even think about medicine...! Which is odd, since we were in a pharmacy," Olivia laughs.

"Well, we should probably head back to the courthouse. Hopefully Jeffrey and everyone else are okay, and all the zombies left." Jeremy leads the way, and we follow behind him.

I'm not sure how long I can deal with Jeffrey's death and not tell anyone. Every time someone mentions him, my eyes swell up, and I think I'm going to have a mental breakdown. I know I'm eventually going to have to tell Jeremy, but I'm not planning on telling him anytime soon.

Chapter 29:

<u>Back at the Courthouse</u>

We arrive at the county government complex, and it looks deserted.

"The zombies did a number on this place," I utter as I pick up a piece of what was once a door.

The cops and politicians that once surrounded this place are nowhere in sight. There's a couple of dead bodies (people and zombies), and I hold my stomach, trying not to throw up.

"I wouldn't recommend looking to the right, if I were you," I advise.

Olivia immediately turns her head away, heeding my warning. "Got it."

"Our group has to be somewhere around here." Jeremy continues walking around the complex.

"Maybe, but what if they ran away just like us?" I counter.

Olivia lets out a loud huff. "You're probably right. Let's just check inside the courthouse first."

As I walk inside the building, an unsettling feeling fills me. It's so eerie being in here after what happened. *No sign of zombies and no sign of anyone else* (If you don't include the dead bodies). Olivia and Jeremy are following closely behind.

"Hello? Anyone here?"

Jeremy immediately covers my mouth with his hand. "Sh…!"

He's right. I better keep it down in case any zombies are still here.

We continue walking ahead and refrain from any conversation. We don't want to alert any zombies that may be lurking nearby. The only sound we can hear are our footsteps, and the constant heavy breathing coming from Jeremy. As we quicken our pace, the floor starts squeaking below our feet, and a voice erupts out of the silence.

"Guys!"

I turn my head around, and it's none other than Reese!

Olivia beams. "You're okay, Reese!"

242

He sighs in relief. "I'm glad to know you kids are alive!" He puts his arms around the three of us. "Are you guys alright?"

"Never been better," Olivia sarcastically replies while holding her thumb up.

Jeremy shrugs. "We're alive, so I can't sulk too much."

I nod.

Reese relaxes a little and leans on the wall. "Well, I'm glad you kids are—"

"Reese, is Jeffrey here?" Jeremy interrupts.

I lower my head and stare at the floor.

"I'm sure he's fine, but no, I haven't seen him." Reese makes eye contact with me and wrinkles his forehead.

Jeremy sighs. "I hope you're right..."

Olivia taps her chin, then makes an *aha* face. "Jeremy, how about we leave him a note!"

"A note?" he asks, intrigued.

"Yeah! We can tell him that we're heading to your parents' house!"

Jeremy thinks for a moment. "I guess that makes sense…But maybe we should stay just a little bit longer? Just in case he comes back."

"Sure, as long as you need," she smiles.

I walk outside and feel the cool summer breeze on my face. I can't bear to hear Olivia and Jeremy talk about Jeffrey any longer. I feel like a bomb waiting to go off at any moment.

Reese catches up to me and observes my behavior for a second before placing his arm around my shoulder. "I know tensions are high because of everything that's going on, but I know something's bothering *you* especially."

How does he know?! Is it that obvious…? I guess I've never been good at hiding my emotions.

Reese tosses a few chips in his mouth. "So, what's up?"

"Jeffrey is dead." The words come out faster and much harsher than I anticipate.

Reese chokes on a chip and starts coughing. "He's what…?" His voice gets lower, until I can barely make out what he's saying. "What happened to the kid?"

244

I feel my eyes getting watery, but I keep the tears inside. *I have to be strong for myself.*

"It was my fault."

Reese takes a breath. "Look Axel, you shouldn't blame yourself. Maybe you could have done something differently, but you're just a kid. This is an insane, unprecedented time for anyone, especially kids."

"But I chose to save Olivia over him...I saw the zombies surrounding him, but it all happened so fast..."

Reese stays quiet for a couple of seconds.

I bet he's realizing how terrible of a person I am.

"You can't have that weight on your shoulders. I'm sure it's hard since Jeremy keeps bringing him up, but at the end of the day, it was a scary situation." He eats a few more potato chips.

"I get what you're saying, but I can't just forgive myself. It's my fault, and I take full responsibility," I express, while staring at the ground beneath my dirty white sneakers.

"I guess you're right, but it's not fair to blame yourself like that. I'm glad you were able to save one of them and didn't run away like a scaredy cat." He finishes his last chip and pats my hat. "Anyone else would've done the same."

I stay silent. *He's right*, I can't keep this weight on my shoulders…I don't know why it was so easy to tell Reese, but so difficult to tell Olivia. I guess Olivia can be judgmental, and I don't really need that right now. Plus, since he's an adult, it's easier to talk to him.

"Oh, and one more thing, your friends Weston and Willow are over there by the lake." Reese strolls back inside the courthouse.

I walk past the building and head to the lake to meet up with Weston and Willow. I turn the corner and watch as Weston and Willow throw rocks across the lake.

"Hey guys…"

Weston turns around and his eyes widen as he sees me. "Axel, you're alive!" He drops the rock in his hand and puts his hand on my shoulder. "Oh, there's Olivia and Jeffrey…Or is it Jeremy?" He looks past me.

I don't have to look behind. Jeffrey's gone, so it has to be Jeremy.

"It's probably Jeremy," I respond as I let out a sigh.

Weston shifts his focus back to me. "And how can you be so sure?"

"I arrived here with Jeremy and Olivia, so I'm willing to bet that's him."

"Oh," he relaxes his shoulders. "I can't tell the difference between them."

"They have different voices, and Jeremy wears glasses."

Weston squints his eyes. "I'm probably still gonna forget who's who," he joked.

Willow elbows her brother. "This is no time for jokes, Wes. We need to figure out a plan."

Weston mutters something under his breath. "I guess you're right. So, Axel, where are we headed now? Most of our plans have been a bust, so I'm out of ideas."

I pick up a rock and toss it in the river. "Well, Olivia and I are going to Michigan."

Willow tilts her head to the side. "Michigan? Why Michigan?"

I tell them about the cabin and all the supplies that will be there. I left out no details.

Weston bends down and touches the water flowing in the river. "It might be best for us to go with you guys. I want to make sure Willow's safe, and if that means going all the way to Michigan, then that's what we'll do."

I smile. "Sounds like a plan."

Reese casually approaches us. "While you kids rest, I'll be trying to hotwire some of these cars parked around here. One is bound to work." He walks over to a truck and opens the door.

I follow Reese to the truck and lean on the car door.

He looks for keys to the truck, but he doesn't find any. "Maybe I can hotwire it..." He lets out a loud groan. "Oh, never mind." He bangs his head on the steering wheel.

"What's wrong?" I inquire.

He lets out an aggravated sigh before responding. "I forgot that new cars have ignition mobilizers now."

I stare at him, clueless. I don't know much about cars. Usually, dads or grandfathers teach their sons and grandsons about cars, but we all know what happened with my dad (if you've been paying attention, you know the sob story), so he didn't teach me. My grandpa on my mom's side is pretty lazy when it comes to mechanics or fixing anything, so I never learned from him. My family on my dad's side doesn't know I exist, so therefore, my other grandpa never taught me anything.

"What's an ignition mobilizer?" I wonder.

He raises his eyebrow. "An ignition mobilizer is…" He pauses. "You know what? Never mind. It just makes hot-wiring cars exceedingly difficult," he replies. "Nearly impossible."

"Which means if these cars don't have keys in them—"

"We aren't going anywhere. Not anytime soon, anyway," he finishes as he searches for the car keys again.

I walk around the truck and open the passenger door. I dust the crumbs off the seat and sit down. "Well, not to change the subject or anything, but did Olivia tell you where we're headed?"

Reese nods his head. "Yeah, she did."

"So, does that mean you're coming with us?"

He smiles at my question. "Yup. We're a group now, right? We have to stick together."

"Yeah, we do."

I can see Olivia and Weston arguing in the rearview mirror.

Great, what is it now?

I get out of the truck and walk over to them. "What's going on?"

Olivia flips her curly hair out of her face. "Well, we never got to finish our conversation about the leader."

I roll my eyes. I should've known Oli would bring this back up. *She loves being in charge.*

I take a deep breath. "Okay, fine. Oli, why do you want to be leader?" I ask.

Olivia ponders on the thought for a moment. There are many reasons that are probably flooding through her mind on why she would want to be the leader. She takes her pointer finger and begins to make her list as she's counting down with each finger.

"First of all, who was the president of the chorus club back at home? ME! Who was the president of the science club? ME! And who was the leader of the book club from middle school on up into high school? Yup, you guessed it, ME! I'm a born leader, Axel. You of all people sh- ould know that," she responds in an arrogant tone.

Weston snickers. "Wow! The president of every dork club wants to lead a survival group! Just so you know, we aren't going to be doing math problems or reading about Sh- akespeare," he provokes.

Great, I guess Weston didn't forget the rude stuff Oli- via said about him earlier inside the courthouse.

Olivia's face instantly turns red. "Who do you think you're talking to? I am not someone you can just make jokes about and think I'm going to sit in a corner and cry about it!"

Weston holds his stomach as he tries to hold in his laughs. "Good for you! You don't seem affected AT ALL by what I said," he sarcastically replies as he claps his hands. "Now, do you want someone that's the leader of um," he cl- ears his throat, "school clubs, or do you want someone like me that's a dead shot?"

Jeremy joins us and puts his thumb and index finger in his mouth and whistles EXTREMELY loud.

I cover my ears. "Seriously?"

"Sorry! I did not realize it would be that loud!" Jeremy points at both Olivia and Weston. "Can you two stop?"

I put my hand on Jeremy's shoulder. "Not to interrupt, but I think Reese should be leader. He's the only adult here, and he clearly has more experience with things like this." I point at Reese hard at work trying to get the truck started.

Jeremy nods. "I agree, studies have shown that—"

Weston interjects. "We get it, Jeremy. But fine, I'll set aside my pride."

Olivia rolls her eyes and briskly walks away.

Chapter 30:

<u>Is Anyone Home?</u>

"Can you turn the AC on? I feel like an egg being fried," Olivia complains as she fans herself with her hand.

The only car that had the key fob in it was a small Toyota Camry that only seats five, so we were basically FIGHTING over the passenger seat. But somehow, Olivia's the one sitting in the passenger seat and still managing to complain about the AC.

Since there's only three seats in the back row, the rest of us: Jeremy, Weston, myself, and Willow, had to squeeze ourselves into those backseats with barely any room to spare.

"I think it would make more sense if the condescending loser that we all call Olivia wasn't sitting in the passenger seat like an evil queen on her throne. A guy should've sat there. There'd be more room back here if one of us did," Weston explains while sitting between Willow and I.

"At least you don't have a window seat like me and Axel. It's awful," Jeremy replies.

253

Weston and Willow share the middle seat, while Jeremy and I are on either side of them.

"Can you guys quit complaining? Gosh." Olivia lets out a quiet chuckle as she finishes her sentence.

Reese grunts. "You guys should be grateful we're not walking."

I glance out the window and surprisingly nothing's in the street except for a few abandoned cars, but no people or zombies (thank goodness).

Olivia puts her feet on the dashboard. "Yeah, be grateful, guys."

Willow squirms. "Easy for you to say, you have a comfortable seat all to yourself." She kicks Olivia's seat.

Willow and Olivia bicker back and forth, and Jeremy quickly cuts them off and his eyes beam.

"THAT'S MY NEIGHBORHOOD!" he exclaims as he points to a neighborhood on the left.

Reese immediately makes a sharp left turn, causing us to slide to the right and crash into one another.

"Ouch…" I take my hat off and rub the back of my head.

"Yikes, Axel. You have some serious hat hair," Olivia laughs as she points at my matted down hair.

"Well, in a survival situation, looking good is not the first thing I think about," I mumble as I pick my hair with my hand.

Willow glances out the window. "Which house is yours, Jeremy?"

He stares at the homes intently. "That one!"

He points to a white, two-story home with a wraparound porch. There's a sign hanging on the front door that reads: '*Home is where the love is.*'

Just as Reese pulls into the driveway, Jeremy pushes the car door open and races for the front door.

He turns the knob aggressively. "Locked!"

"Please tell me you guys don't keep the spare key under the mat?" Weston groans as he steps out of the car.

I open the car door and stretch my arms and legs. This neighborhood sounds unusually quiet. I can almost imagine how lively it was before the plague we call zombies hit. Little kids using the sprinkler in the scorching summer heat, mothers explaining how they can't wait 'till school's back in session. Fathers—

Olivia interrupts my thoughts. "Axel! Jeremy got the door open, come on! We don't want anything to spot us!" She enters the home.

"Coming!" I sprint to the front door and step inside, and the home looks ransacked! Furniture is thrown around, and the pantry and fridge are wide open with barely any food left.

"Be vigilant everyone. Whoever caused this could still be around here," Reese whispers as he pulls out his gun.

I nod and look around the living space. Unlike Weston's house, there aren't many photos hanging on the wall, just one. The picture shows a woman with golden blonde hair and tan skin wearing a stunning wedding dress. Beside her stood a white man almost twice her height with short black hair, wearing a pearl white suit. *Those are probably Jeremy's parents.*

Weston interrupts my thoughts and starts flicking a light switch on and off. "Hey! The lights don't work. Maybe the power went out over here, too."

Reese flips a different light switch on, but no luck. "That might be the case. Hopefully they get the power back up and running soon."

256

Jeremy enters the room with a gloomy expression on his face. He holds a small sheet of paper in his hand.

"What's wrong?" I ask.

"My parents left a letter…They said that they got bit by a zombie, and they were on their way to the hospital. They said they love me and Jeff very m-much…" He falls to the ground and holds his hands over his face, whimpering.

All I can think about is Jeffrey. Jeremy lost everyone he loved; his twin brother and now both of his parents. He still has a false hope that Jeffrey's okay, but I know he's gone… And he's never coming back.

Weston sits down beside him and everyone follows.

"I'm sorry, Jeremy. I know showing my condolences doesn't fix anything but knowing that people are here for you will help you cope," Weston encourages. He then gets up and walks out of the house.

I guess Weston is the only person that can relate to Jeremy right now. They both lost their parents (Weston losing only one).

257

"Yeah, and you and Jeffrey will reunite soon, too. I'm just sure of it! If you need more time to stay here, you're more than welcome too," Olivia tells him.

I look behind me and see Reese scribbling something on a sheet of paper. "Hey guys! I think I found something!" He races to Jeremy and hands him the sheet of paper.

Jeremy reads the paper and lets out a sigh. "I'm glad he's okay, but…why didn't he just wait for me?"

I stare at him in confusion. *Is he talking about Jeffrey?* I snatch the paper from Jeremy's hand.

"Hey!" Jeremy folds his arms in frustration.

"Hey, had to go quickly. I'm heading to the cabin in Michigan. Hopefully you know what I'm talking about. Love you."

-Jeffrey

Yup. Just as I suspected, it's a letter from "Jeffrey". But I know he died, and I also know I saw Reese writing on that sheet of paper. *Is he helping me?*

Jeremy takes the paper from my hand. "Wait a second." He takes his glasses off, easing the paper closer to his face. "This handwriting is so neat, he's usually very messy when he writes." He squints his eyes hard.

I start pacing back in forth. *Oh great, he's gonna know. He's gonna know.*

Reese scratches the back of his head. "Well, uh, maybe he wanted to make sure this letter was readable!"

Jeremy shrugs. "Maybe."

Reese mumbles under his breath. "If that's neat, he should see me write when I'm not in a rush."

It seems like I'm the only one that heard him, because no one else reacted.

Olivia looks at the paper. "How did he know about the cabin?" She puts her hand on her chin.

I give Olivia the death glare and she just looks in confusion.

"He may or may not have overheard us talking about it," I shrug. "I mean, we were talking about it at the courthouse."

Olivia puts her finger on her chin and twists her mouth. "Hm."

Jeremy sets the paper down on the table. "Well, I guess I'll be heading to Michigan then. I just wish he waited for me…That's not like him." He opens the front door and walks to the car.

Reese and I share a look. I feel so bad, but if I told him the truth, he'd hate me. So much has happened in such a short amount of time. First, Weston's mom turned into a zombie…*Rest in peace*…then Rob turned…*I miss you bud*…then Jeffrey died…*I'm sorry*…and now Jeremy's parents turned. I just hope things go back to normal soon, because I'm not sure how much more of this I can deal with.

I step outside the house and pull Weston to the side. "Can I talk to you and Willow for a sec?"

He wrinkles his forehead and brings Willow over. "What's up?"

I take a deep breath. "I don't think I ever told you guys that I'm sorry for your loss."

"Our loss?" he asks.

"Yeah. So much happened after Rob got bit. I never told you and Willow that I was sorry about what happened to your mom."

Willow and Weston remain silent for a minute. Then Weston pulls me into a hug with him and Willow.

"Thanks man, that means a lot." He wipes his eyes (though, I didn't see any tears).

Willow nods her head and squeezes her brother's arm. "Yeah, thank you. You're the only one who's actually said that."

I smile at them both. It feels good giving my condolences, especially since everyone else is too busy to give theirs.

Chapter 31:
<u>Two Months Later</u>

Honestly with all that's been going on, I've started to lose track of time. I think we've been on the road for about two months or so, because I've been trying to keep track of when the sun sets and rises (well, I do sometimes). Luckily Jeremy's parents owned a van and the spare key was on the dashboard. So, we took the van, and we were on our way to Michigan (we knew we couldn't ride comfortably all the way to Michigan in a small Toyota).

At first, we were using the GPS to lead us to the cabin. I just put the address in the car's system (since mom told me to know it by heart), and we were off. But the GPS kept glitching, so that's what started delaying us.

And to make matters worse, the van broke down! So, we've been walking the rest of the way (which has been awful). What's even worse is that we have to rely on a map to get us the rest of the way, but none of us are great at reading it.

"KILL IT!" Jeremy screams as he holds a zombie inches from his face.

Olivia shoots the male zombie in the arm with the crossbow, sticking his arm to the grass. "There. Now it won't bother you, or anyone for that matter."

Jeremy puts both his hands on Olivia's shoulders. "What took you so long to shoot? I was almost dead, because of you!"

She pushes his hands off her. "Don't touch me!" She briskly walks ahead of him. "Plus, it's not like I was the ONLY one that could have helped!" She points at me and Reese.

Jeremy picks his bag up from off the ground. "Reese and Axel are ahead of us, and Willow and Weston are behind us! You were the only one close enough to help!"

"Just shush! A thank you would suffice!"

We're walking along the side of a highway, so it's harder for anything to sneak up on us. We tried going through the woods at first, but we had too many close calls with animals and zombies.

Reese shakes his head. "They are so childish."

I nod at his remark and change the subject. "How long till we get to the cabin?"

Reese shrugs his shoulders as he stares at the map. "Who knows? This stupid map isn't doing us any justice now. We've been constantly stopping to look for supplies, sleeping, and having to take different routes to avoid dangerous situations. I have no idea where we are anymore."

He stops in his tracks and folds the map. "I'm sorry Axel, but we might need to go back South. It's starting to get really cold. Maybe we should try again in a few months when fall and winter are over."

"We did not come all this way for nothing!" Olivia snaps, then looks at me for support. "We have come too far to just turn back now! Our parents want us to keep going, right Axel?"

I want to say yes. I want to tell her that that's what they want us to do. But right now, as I look at everyone, I'm starting to think I made a mistake. Bringing all these people with us...and for what? I don't even know if our parents made it to the cabin. Heck, I don't even know if they're alive. But do I really want Olivia to know about my fear? *My fear of all of this being for nothing?*

As I contemplate what to say, I decide to tell Olivia what she wants to hear. *What I want to believe.* "Yeah, we should keep going—"

"Guys, I see snowflakes!" Weston points at the snowflakes falling from the sky.

"This is gonna be bad..." I mumble as the snowflakes start falling faster.

Jeremy stares at the sky. "That's so weird that it's snowing in September! It's not usually this cold in Michigan around this time."

Reese squints his eyes and scans the area for a place to stay. "We need to find shelter while this snowstorm passes."

Willow points to an abandoned gas station not too far from where we're standing. "We should go there!"

"Let's go!" I shout.

I sprint to the gas station, not wasting any time. I can hear the rest of the group's feet stomping on the concrete as we race to the building.

I reach the gas station first, and the rest of the group arrives soon after me.

"This place looks intimidating," Weston mumbles.

He's right. The windows are broken, and the paint looks faded. There are also blood stains on the front door!

"Maybe we should take our chances out here. Less chance of...*death*," Olivia playfully titters, but I can hear the nervousness in her voice.

"But if we stay out here, we could get sick. And if you haven't noticed, medicine is hard to come by," Willow explains in a demeaning tone while brushing past Olivia. "I'm heading inside."

"Like brother like sister," Olivia mumbles under her breath.

Weston swings his head around and glares at her. "What was that?"

"I don't repeat myself." And with that, Olivia follows Willow inside.

Me and Reese exchange the *what-is-everyone's-problem* look and follow behind the rest of the group.

Jeremy steps inside and starts rubbing his arms. "It's chilly in here."

"Ooh! A hat!" Olivia picks up a pink cap and dusts the dirt off it. "It's cute!" She puts the hat on her head and grins.

Reese looks around and makes sure there aren't any zombies or people lurking around. "I don't think anyone's here."

The gas station is a small building with a few aisles. There's a ton of empty packages of food scattered across the floor. *This place must have been raided a while ago.*

"Yeah, I don't think anyone's here either." I notice snow making its way inside through two broken windows. "Now we know why it's super cold in here," I conclude.

Willow folds her arms in frustration. "Just perfect."

Weston looks out the window (well, what once was a window), and points at a few zombies. "Hey guys, check out the zombies. They're really slow."

I watch as the zombies slowly drag their feet across the snowy terrain.

Jeremy sits on the cold floor. "It's probably because it's so cold…"

Olivia's eyes widen for a moment. She eases closer to the window and points in surprise. "Look! Some are even falling…"

Out of nowhere, she starts breathing heavily, and she crashes to the ground!

Reese immediately helps her off the ground. "Woah, are you alright, Olivia?"

She leans on the counter and lets out a raspy cough. "Not really…"

I zip her jacket all the way up. As I do, I realize that she looks lethargic. "You don't look so good, Oli."

"Well, that's 'cause I *don't* feel good. To be honest, I haven't been feeling that great for a couple days," she admits.

I look at her in shock. "And you didn't say anything to me?"

Reese waves his hand in the air, signaling for me to stop talking. "Axel, do you have any more medicine in your bag?"

I grab my bookbag and unzip it. "I'll check."

When we went to the pharmacy a few months back, I found some medicine. Hopefully I'll find something that can reduce her symptoms.

I search through my bag and find pain medicine. *It won't help with reducing the symptoms, but it will help ease any pain.*

Weston lifts Olivia off the ground and lays her on the counter.

Olivia grunts as she turns on her side. "I didn't need a knight in shining armor to carry me to safety," she mumbles.

Weston leans over the counter. "I honestly could have done without that comment."

Olivia remains quiet for a few seconds, then sighs deeply. "Please be honest with me, Weston. Did you set Rob up? Did you want him to die?"

Weston's face switches from his usual cocky demeaner to a more serious expression. "Of course not! You already heard the story! There would be no reason why I'd want Rob dead!" Weston's eyes fill with water. "What gain would I have? Why would I deliberately plan all of that?" His voice cracks as he finishes.

Willow stands in front of her brother and leans toward Olivia. "Yeah! My brother was just looking out for our mom! Leave him alone!"

Olivia, taken aback, shifts her gaze to the floor. "I'm sorry…! I should have known you didn't want anything to happen to Rob. I just…I don't know…"

Weston puts his hands on Olivia's shoulders and takes a deep breath. "It's okay. So much has happened anyway, I won't hold a grudge," he forces a smile (and, if I'm not mistaken, I'm pretty sure I saw a tear roll down his cheek).

Olivia lets out a sigh of relief and nods her head. "Thank you."

Willow cuts her eyes at Olivia and storms off, still mad that Olivia accused her brother of something so heinous.

I can't blame her.

Reese interrupts the conversation by placing his hand on Oli's forehead. "Well, the good news is, you don't have a fever. The bad news is, you're freezing. You probably just have a cold," he reassures.

"Oh, that's good," Olivia replies, as she watches Weston make his way over to Willow on the other side of the gas station.

270

I lean my back up against the wall. "Yeah, that's good, but we need you to get warm. You don't need to get worse."

Oli just shrugs her shoulders and observes Weston and Willow from afar.

Reese opens the security room and looks around. "I was hoping to find something we could use, but there's nothing useful in here."

Jeremy squeezes beside Reese and explores the security room as well. "If we could find a portable heater it would make all the difference."

"A portable heater? It'd be easier to find a needle in a haystack," Reese responds, as he tosses a few empty boxes of cheese squares on the floor. "We might be able to find a few things to start a fire, though."

Weston makes his way back over to us and chuckles softly. "Reese, where are we going to make a fire? Inside the gas station and burn the place to bits? Or outside, where the snow would kill the fire before it even starts?"

Reese raises his finger in the air. "See, you always try to—"

"Guys, Look! Smoke is coming from that chimney!" Jeremy points his finger at a house in the distance.

I look in awe at the smoke coming from a house not too far from here.

"We should go there! Maybe someone can help us!" I blurt out.

Reese raises both his hands in the air. "Wait, we can't all go. Weston and I should go."

Weston slams his hand on the countertop. "No! I need to look after my sister!"

"Yeah, he looks out for me," Willow dryly responds.

I nod in agreement. "I agree. Also, Reese, you're the only adult here, so you need to stay with Olivia in case something happens."

Reese nervously taps his right foot on the ground. "But who's gonna go instead?"

"I'll go!" I open the front door and step out of the gas station before anyone can rebuttal. I try to move as fast as I can, so I don't freeze like an icicle.

"It's really cold out here," Jeremy comments, taking me out of my thoughts.

I turn my head around.

No! I don't want Jeremy to come! I don't want anything to happen to him.

"You don't have to come, you know."

"Yeah, I know. But we're a team! You shouldn't go by yourself."

I guess he has a point.

I reluctantly nod my head and pick up the pace. "The house is about a mile from the gas station, so we're probably going to get there in a few minutes," I explain.

"Technically, it takes most people about eleven minutes to complete a mile run, or at least me, so we'll get there in about fifteen minutes. Since it's really cold and we're not walking as fast," he responds in a matter-of-fact tone.

"Well then, let's pick up the pace a little more."

Chapter 32:

<u>The Stranger</u>

We arrive at the small house and Jeremy stares at it in fear. The house has a gray outer coat, with a steel fence surrounding the property. There's also a large tree that is casting a cryptic shadow on the snow.

"This place gives me MAJOR horror movie vibes," he whispers, shivering at the house's presence.

I let a low chuckle. "Ha, you sound like Rob…" I stop in my tracks. *I can't believe I slipped up like that.* With all the challenges these past months, I developed a habit of forgetting about those that were lost…Well, I guess I wouldn't call it forgetting, more like trying to keep the memories of them in a distant place in my mind.

"I'm sorry, I didn't mean to bring him up," I mumble, feeling stupid.

Jeremy stares at me, then laughs uncontrollably. He drops to the ground and rolls on his side, hollering.

"Is this the way you cope with loss?" I frown.

I'm starting to worry about his wellbeing.

Once Jeremy gets himself together, he lets out one last chuckle before replying. "You really made my day, you know that?"

I stare at him blankly. I thought he would have been upset or mad that I brought Rob up. "I'm confused," I admit.

Jeremy sits crisscrossed on the ground. "I never think about those I've lost." He closes his eyes. "But that comment you made, whether it was on purpose or not, reminded me that I shouldn't forget those I've lost along the way, especially Rob. He was a good kid, and I think he'd prefer us talking about him more." He opens his eyes, and they meet with mine.

I guess he's right. We shouldn't forget about them. They were all good people and deserve to be remembered. Jeremy deserves to know about his brother, too. I know he'll probably hate me, but I can't keep this from him any longer.

"Jeremy...I have to tell you something—"

The door to the house swings open, and a man around 6'5 with a full-grown beard, white skin, and blonde hair steps out. Before looking at us, he spits on the ground below him. "Whatcha boys doin' here?"

275

He has the thickest country accent I think I've ever heard. Maybe an Alabama accent.

"Um. We were w-wondering if…" Jeremy stands up and slowly backs away.

I don't know how he managed to sit on the snow like that. It's way too cold.

"Look sir, we are just two guys that need our friend taken care of," I tell him as I try to hold my fear inside.

The man cracks his knuckles and talks in a low tone. "What kind of taken care of? The kind where you *never* have to worry 'bout 'em again?" He raises his bushy eyebrows.

We shiver and shake our heads frantically.

"N-NO! We just want to get her someplace warm. She might be sick, and we don't want her getting worse," I express.

The man turns his head to the right, then to the left and turns his attention back to us. "I don't see no girl," he murmurs while squinting his eyes.

"Well, she's at the gas station over there," I answer, while pointing in the direction of it.

The man rubs his chin with his hand. "Mm…I see. Well, you're more than welcome to bring her here," he suggests.

"Really? Thank you!" Jeremy relaxes a little.

"Yeah, thanks!"

We race back to the gas station as fast as we can, so we can tell our group the good news!

....

We open the door to the gas station and Oli's fast asleep on the counter, Weston's reloading his gun, and Willow's eating a granola bar, but no sign of Reese.

"Do you guys know where Reese is?" I wonder.

Weston cocks back his gun. "He left to look for more supplies."

"Why?" I raise my eyebrow.

Willow takes a bite of her granola bar. "He looked in our bags and realized that we were running low on supplies, so he insisted on leaving."

Weston nods and lays on the floor. "So, I'm assuming no one was at that house?"

"A man lives there, but he told us that we could stay," Jeremy responds.

Weston taps his finger on his gun. "That seems too…easy. That guy might be bad news."

Olivia opens her eyes and lets out a loud yawn. "What's happening?"

I turn my focus to her. "We're heading to the house. Hop on." I bend down, signaling for Oli to get on my back.

"I think I can walk…" she states, while frowning her face.

Even after everything we've been through, Oli still thinks she has to do everything herself.

It's okay to ask for help.

"I think it's best if you take it easy."

Olivia reluctantly hops on my back. "I guess you're right." She feels almost as light as a feather as she positions herself comfortably.

Olivia has always been small. Since she runs track…well, did run track, she always had to maintain a certain weight in order to be the best she can be (so she thinks), but after everything that's happened, she's a lot lighter than she used to be, which is probably because we barely eat anything and run all the time.

"Comfortable?"

"Yup. You sure you can lift me?" she jokes.

"Are you kidding? You're probably the lightest person I've ever carried…And that's including August," I laugh.

Olivia snickers and kicks my leg. "You're such a liar!"

Weston walks over to me. "As much as I hate to disrupt this conversation, I'm not sure if we should go in that house. Like I mentioned before, the man must have an ulterior motive." He puts his arm around Willow.

Jeremy taps his foot on the ground and reaches for the door handle. "Fine. You stay with Willow, while the rest of us scope out the house." He holds the door open for me to grab, and I follow him outside.

Weston keeps the door open with his leg. "Okay, fine. Just be careful."

Jeremy waves at Weston. "We will. But if we're not back in ten minutes, come rescue us!"

"Will do!" He flexes his muscles, showing off his biceps.

"You're not the only person that has muscles, Weston," Olivia mumbles, as I carry her into the snowstorm.

Chapter 33:

Questionable Help

We arrive at the small home and knock on the door, and the man immediately swings the door wide open.

"Welcome back." He steps to the side so we can enter the house.

As we step inside, I look to my left and see three deer heads lying on the ground (not on the wall like they're supposed to). Jeremy gasps and points at a door. The door looks rusted with blood leaking from the bottom of it, and a large lock keeping it shut.

Not gonna lie, the house looks a bit creepy.

Jeremy's lip quivers. "What do you think goes on in there?"

I put my finger to his mouth. "Sh…"

The man glances back at us and wipes his beard. "So, girl, are you alright?" he asks in a cryptic voice as he leads us down the hallway.

Olivia shivers. "Um, y-yeah, I'm fine."

He turns around and smiles (I can see a few teeth missing as he does so). He then stops in his tracks and looks at Jeremy. "I have some food, if you kids want some."

"No thanks!" Jeremy quickly replies.

The man continues pacing forward. He stops once we reach the fireplace at the end of the hallway. "You guys can stay here while I get some pillows." He walks in a different direction and soon disappears into a dark hallway.

Olivia practically jumps off my back! "Okay! This place is freaky and so is that man!"

I scratch the back of my hat. "I don't think he's a bad guy. He's just strange."

Jeremy points his finger at me. "You and I both know you don't believe that!"

Okay, he's kinda right. I'm just trying not to freak out.

Oli looks over at the hallway the man walked down. "Jeremy, you need to lower your voice."

Completely disregarding her comment, Jeremy keeps his attention on me. "And what's up with that creepy door? I bet he's a cannable!"

Olivia's eyes widen at the comment, and she starts biting her bottom lip.

What they're saying is purely speculation, and if they're wrong, we'd be spending the night in a freezing cold gas station instead of a cozy home.

I put my hands on both Jeremy's and Olivia's shoulders. "You know what? Will you guys calm down if I see what's behind the door? It looks super old. I bet I can just break the lock," I offer.

I don't really want to go and explore any creepy places, but Olivia needs to be somewhere safe, and this might be the only way she stays.

"That would make me feel better. Good thing you're not easily frightened," she states.

Jeremy pats me on the back and eases behind Olivia. "Yeah, just yell if you need anything."

I creep down the hallway (since that's where the creepy door is). The wood continuously creeks after each step I take, and if that guy is paying attention, he'll realize that someone is walking around his home…and that won't be good for anyone.

There it is.

I reach my hand for the old, rusty knob. I start turning the doorknob, but it doesn't budge.

"Right, it's locked."

I look around for something to help me break the lock, and I notice a pipe leaning up against the wall. I immediately pick it up and start hitting the lock.

This is such a bad idea.

I swing the pipe one last time, and the lock breaks a little.

"It's working! Just one more time!"

"WHAT ARE YOU DOING?!"

I hear the man's aggressive tone behind me as the floor creaks. I also hear Jeremy and Olivia screaming!

"RUN AXEL!"

As I turn around, I see fury in the man's eyes.

Great.

I take off running past the creepy door and notice another door at the end of the hallway. I quickly turn the knob, but, *since situations like this are never in my favor*, it's also locked.

"Just stop for a moment!" The man shouts as he quickens his pace.

Okay. So, for me to make it back to Jeremy and Oli, I have to pass him. *Baseball mode on.* I'm trying to reach home base, but a fielder is trying to get me out. *Focus Axel...Focus...*

I take off running down the hallway! I need to get past him in order to reach the fireplace, so I have to be quick! He reaches his arms out and tries to grab me, but I dodge him. As I'm almost back to Olivia and Jeremy, the man snags the back of my shirt, and I fall flat on my back.

BAM!

Olivia snatches her crossbow from behind her back and points it at the man. "Don't kill him!"

Jeremy's standing next to Olivia and he's holding a baseball bat in the air, ready to swing. "Yeah, leave him alone!"

I pull my knife out of my pocket in case he tries anything.

285

The man gives Olivia and Jeremy a blank stare. "Why would I wanna kill 'em? I just wanted to know why he was tryna get in the room where I clean the animals I hunt." He extends his hand for me to grab.

I slowly grab it and dust my pants off.

Olivia lowers her bow. "Well, that makes me feel much better."

Jeremy sighs in relief. "Me too."

The man chuckles. "Yeah, I lock that door because there's a lot of sharp tools in there. I didn't want y'all gettin' hurt."

"Well, now I'm just embarrassed," I rub the back of my neck.

The man winks. "Oh, it's alright. I'd be curious too."

"By the way," Jeremy clears his throat, "what's your name?"

The man takes his seat next to the fireplace. "It's Mitch."

. . . .

The fire is keeping us nice and toasty. Mitch seems like a friendly guy, but I'm keeping my guard up just in case. On a lighter note, Oli's getting better by the minute.

KNOCK!

KNOCK!

Olivia turns her head around and stares at the front door. "Someone's at the door."

Mitch nods his head and reaches for his shotgun. "I'll be back." He stands up and eases the door open.

I wait a couple seconds before following Mitch to the door. As I get closer, I can see it's none other than Weston and Willow!

"Weston!" I shout as I see him and Willow shivering on the steps.

Mitch swings his head around. "Friends of yours?"

"Yup. Can they stay the night, too?"

Mitch scratches his head. "I don't see why not. Y'all can join yer crew."

"Thanks, Mitch."

Mitch widens the door and waves his hand for Weston and Willow to come inside. "Show them to the fireplace, will ya?"

I nod at his request. "Sure."

Mitch smiles and disappears into one of the rooms down the hallway.

"So, why'd you guys come? Did something happen?" I ask Weston as I make my way back to the fireplace.

"No," he shrugs. "Jeremy told me that if you guys didn't come back in ten minutes, then I'd need to come and save your butts," Weston retells as he tries to impersonate Jeremy.

I let out a laugh. "You sound nothing like him."

Weston chuckles, then sits down in front of the fire.

Chapter 34:

<u>Out of the Loop</u>

"So, what brings you to this part of the woods? Where are your parents?" Mitch takes a bite of a chicken leg.

Weston licks his fingers and takes a breath. "Well, this guy," he points to me, "has a cabin up here. We're heading there so we can get away from the infected people."

Mitch wrinkles his forehead and sets his chicken on the ground. "Infected people? What are you talking about?"

Me and Weston share a look. *Is this guy crazy or something?*

"Are you joking, Mitch?" I respond.

Mitch leans his head forward. "Am I jokin'? Are you folks jokin'?"

"Are you telling me that you don't know about the virus that's been spreading for months?" Olivia stares at him in disbelief.

Mitch scratches his beard before he answers. "Should I?"

289

"You haven't noticed the lack of traffic around here?" Jeremy interrogates.

"I've lived out in the wilderness of Michigan for over twenty years. The closest thing to me is the gas station a mile up, so I'm used to not seeing people." Mitch stares off in the distance. "I did notice that less and less people go to the gas station, but I figured people didn't want to come all this way for gas."

I can't believe Mitch doesn't know about the outbreak. Is he really off the grid that much that he didn't hear a word about it?

Willow's eyes wander around the house. "So, you don't have a tv or a radio?"

"Nope. I've been off the grid most of my life, but I used to live in Texas. I hunt my own game, and I have a garden in the backyard."

Ah, so it was a Texas accent.

"That's so weird," Willow utters under her breath.

Mitch shakes his head in disbelief. "How bad is the virus?"

We all remain silent. *How bad is the virus?*

290

"Where do we even begin?" I stare at the floor below my feet. "Think of the rabies virus, but a million times worse."

"If an infected person bites you, you turn into one of them in a few hours," Olivia responds.

Mitch's eyes start dilating. "Oh my gosh...I don't know how to process all this." He puts his chicken leg in the trashcan. "I'm sorry, but I don't think it's safe or smart for y'all to stay here. You've already used some of my supplies, and I don't know if any of y'all are infected."

I put both my hands on my head in frustration. "I guess that makes sense...But we aren't infected."

"I don't know that for sure. Y'all can stay the night, but please leave first thing in the morning. I wish I could help more, but I need to figure out what's been going on for months."

For the rest of the night, we beg him to let us stay, but he doesn't budge. I can't say I blame him. *He has a lot to catch up on.*

Chapter 35:

<u>Where's Reese?</u>

Once morning arrived, Mitch told us to be on our way, but he kept apologizing. I can't imagine what he's going through to be honest. Without a rebuttal, I lead our group out the door. As much as I wanted to continue campaigning for our stay, we needed to meet back up with Reese and head to the cabin.

I open the front door of the gas station, and there's a ton of snow inside of it.

"Oh wow! Looks like a snowy wonderland!" Willow stares in shock.

Olivia steps inside and takes a long look around. "Reese, are you in here?" she shouts, but there's no sign of him anywhere.

Weston runs his fingers through the snow on the floor. "Maybe he stayed somewhere for the night, since it snowed so much."

I know I haven't known Reese for very long, but I don't think he'd just stay someplace for the night, knowing that we'd expect him to come back with some supplies.

"What if he's in trouble? I mean, zombies could've gotten him or worse!" I worry.

Willow takes a seat on the snowy floor. "What's worse than zombies? I sure would like to know!" She raises her eyebrow curiously.

I squint my eyes. "Dangerous people."

Jeremy ponders on the thought, then shakes his head. "I don't think so. I mean, there's been dangerous people on this Earth since the beginning of time, and we've never had to survive like this before."

"I guess that makes sense, but I just want to make sure he's alright." I make my way through the thick snow and sit on the counter.

Olivia puts her hands on her hips. "You don't mean you're actually going back out in that awful weather, right?"

I lean my hands back. "That's exactly what I mean!"

Jeremy claps his hands. "He's right, Olivia. We have to look for Reese!"

"*We?* You're coming, too?" I'm taken back.

Jeremy puts his arm around my shoulder. "Yeah! We're a team, and we look out for each other. Reese has done a lot for us, and there's no reason why I shouldn't look for him!"

Out of nowhere, I feel a tugging on my arm from behind the counter! I turn my head around and a zombie is pulling my arm toward its mouth!

"AHH! LET GO!" I aggressively try to pull my arm back.

"AXEL!" Olivia screams.

I don't know if it's in my head or not, but it feels like everything is going ten times slower. The more I pull away from the zombie, the slower time feels to go, and the tighter the zombie's grip begins to feel. I slowly close my eyes and pull with all my might!

BANG!

I open my eyes and Jeremy's gun is smoking. He...He saved my life!

I quickly back away from the counter and look at my right arm.

Thank goodness it didn't bite me!

Olivia wraps her arms around me. "I thought you were going to get bit!"

"It's okay Oli, I'm fine." I give Jeremy a hug. "Thank you, Jer! You saved me!" As soon as the words leave my mouth, I remember that I couldn't save his brother...

Jeremy beams. "Why the long face, Axel? I get you almost got bit and all, but you're safe now."

"It's just..." I look at the floor.

I can't even look at him.

Willow's eyes fill with water. "I can't imagine how you feel, Axel. You couldn't save his—" Willow immediately covers her mouth, and I cover her hands.

"Anyway, thanks, Jeremy!" I smile nervously.

"Okay then," Jeremy shrugs his shoulders and heads outside.

Weston snatches my hand from Willow's face. "Why did you cover my sister's face like that?" He then stares at Willow. "And what were you going to say?"

Me and Willow make eye contact, and I clear my throat. I'm guessing he's not going to wait much longer for me to give an explanation before he blows.

"Jeffrey's…Jeffrey's dead."

Weston's eyes widen and so do Olivia's. She covers her mouth in despair.

"W-What are you talking about, man?" Weston's voice cracks.

I sit on the floor and close my eyes, reliving the horror that I've been trying to hide all these weeks. "Back at the courthouse, Jeffrey was surrounded by zombies. He yelled my name…looked right at me, but Olivia was in danger too…"

A tear rolls down my cheek. "I saved her instead. I tried convincing myself that anyone would have saved the person they care about more, but I don't know. It doesn't make it hurt any less or make me feel less guilty." By the time I finish retelling the situation, tears are rolling down my face.

Willow sits next to me. "Yeah, I saw it all happen…Weston was pulling me out of the building, but I was able to see Jeffrey shouting your name and Olivia trapped between zombies." She wipes her nose. "I didn't say anything because I knew why you did what you did. You had to save your best friend."

Olivia clenches her fists. "If I wasn't some stupid damsel in distress, you could have saved him!"

I shake my head. "Olivia, please don't do that. I made the decision, no one else."

Weston lets out a loud huff. "Axel...It's no one's fault. Plus, my situation was much worse."

I raise my eyebrow. "What do you mean?"

"A while back, remember when that zombie...my mom...almost bit Willow?"

"Yeah, I remember that."

"Me too..." Olivia utters.

Weston clears his throat and leans on the counter. "Well, I couldn't save my own sister. MY OWN SISTER! A zombie was going to bite her, and for the first time, I didn't feel so superior. I needed help, but I was still too prideful to admit it." He puts his arms around Willow. "I almost lost everything I'm fighting for, and now, I'll forever be in debt to

Rob. I'll never forget him." He pulls Willow to his chest. *"I'll never forget him."*

He's right. He's the only one that understands. Two people that we cared about died, and we both could've prevented that. It stings every time I think about it, but I'm just glad I have someone that can relate to me.

"Thank you, Weston."

"No problem, Axel. Don't be so hard on yourself. Trust me, that helps no one." He lets go of Willow and pats my hat.

Willow looks up at her brother. "I love you, Weston."

Weston smiles embarrassingly. "Yeah, yeah, I know." He ruffles her hair.

Willow's face lights up.

They are so adorable.

Olivia hugs me. "Back to the topic at hand, Weston's right, Axel. We're never going to forget about Jeffrey. He was amazing, but you can't blame yourself for something that zombies did. You saved my life, and I'm forever grateful. Don't beat yourself up because you couldn't save him too."

Everyone's being so supportive. This would've helped me earlier when I was so stressed. I didn't have to deal with it on my own, but I'm glad to know that I can count on these guys like a real family. And yeah, Jeffrey and Rob will never be forgotten.

"Let's just not mention this to Jeremy, I doubt he'll be as supportive and understanding as us," Weston responds.

I agree. "Yeah, I think it's best that way."

Olivia watches Jeremy walk back toward the door. "But we do need to tell him eventually, right?"

I pace back and forth. "Yeah, eventually."

Jeremy flings the door wide open and races inside. "I can see a town a little way from here! If Reese was seeking shelter, or needs help, he'll probably be there!"

There's no point in everyone risking their lives. Some of us can stay if they want.

"Everyone doesn't have to come," I explain.

Willow tugs on Weston's sleeve. "Wes, I'm going to stay."

Weston shakes his head. "No, you need to come along. I'm gonna help Axel and Jeremy, and I don't feel comfortable being away from you."

Willow wrinkles her forehead. "I don't need protecting! I can take care of myself!" She stomps her foot.

"I know, but I'd feel more comfortable if you'd come along with me, so I can look after you."

Weston says it like a request, but I don't think he's really asking her to come along, *he's telling her to.*

Olivia chimes in. "I could stay with her. I'm responsible. Not to brag, but I use to have my very own babysitting company!"

Olivia said, "Not to brag", but she doesn't mind boasting about anything she's good at.

Willow looks up at her brother. "I don't need a babysitter!"

Weston groans. "Don't be difficult Willow, and thanks Olivia, but I don't know if I feel that comfortable."

Olivia steps closer to Weston. "I promise I will guard her with my life." She looks Weston in the eyes with affirmation.

Weston puts his hands on Olivia's shoulders. "Okay, fine. Nothing better happen to her." He ruffles Willow's hair again and leaves the gas station.

As I step outside the building, I look up at the sky. The clouds are covering the sun to the point where I can barely see it. The temperature is dropping by the millisecond, and my hands are beginning to freeze.

"I can barely see anything in all this snow! Are you sure this is the right way, Jeremy?" I hold my hand in front of my face as I try to make my way through the snow.

"I think so...or maybe not? Just keep going straight, I'm sure we'll see it!" Jeremy reassures.

"Maybe it's not smart to keep walking in a random direction! We might get lost!" Weston shouts, trying to hear himself over the loud whistling of the wind.

I can't see anything! I lift both of my hands up, but I'm not able to see them in front of my face!

"Weston, Axel, we should probably just turn back!" Jeremy exclaims.

I can hear Jeremy's voice ahead of me, but I can't see him at all.

"Jeremy? Weston? Where are you guys?" I slowly walk forward, hoping I don't bump into anything.

"I don't know where I am! I can't see a thing," Weston mumbles.

The cold is penetrating my skin. If I didn't know any better, I would've thought I wasn't wearing a coat at all! I collapse to the ground and feel the freezing snow at my fingertips. "Guys…I can't go any further, it's too cold!" I wait for a response, but the howling wind is the only thing that seems to have heard me. "GUYS?" I shout, in hopes that one of them will hear me.

I lay down on the snowy ground, unable to move any further. I slowly close my eyes, realizing that there's no hope for me, and I soon fall into a deep slumber.

Chapter 36:

<u>Mysterious Saviors</u>

My eyes slowly open as I regain consciousness.

"Where...Where am I?"

I look around and realize that I'm no longer in the freezing snow; I'm in a bedroom. The bedroom has a bed (which I'm currently on), a few nature photos framed on the wall, and two doors. There are also a few candles lit up on the nightstand beside the bed.

"How did I get here?" I stand up and I'm no longer wearing my black long-sleeved shirt and blue jeans, but instead, I'm wearing red shorts and a white short-sleeved shirt. I frantically look around for my coat, but it's nowhere in sight.

I scratch my head in confusion and realize I don't have my hat on either! I head over to one of the doors.

"I hope this leads to the exit."

Don't get me wrong, whoever brought me here is really nice and all, but I don't want to stay here any longer than I have to.

I slowly open a red door, and it leads to a closet. A small closet with nothing in it. I close the door back and walk over to the other one. As I reach my hand toward the doorknob, it turns, and the door pushes open.

I step back from the door, so I don't get hit.

A woman with pale skin and a short brown haircut walks into the room. "Oh, dear, I didn't mean to startle you!" She smiles, then pushes a few strands of hair behind her ear.

"Uh, don't worry about it. But um, where am I?"

As the woman smiles, her pearly white teeth shimmer in the dim room. "Oh! You're at me and my husband's estate!"

I slowly nod, not really feeling any assurance. "How did I get here?" I probe.

She lets out a loud, forced laugh. "HA! You're very inquisitive, aren't you? How about I explain everything over a nice cup of tea?"

I look at her with a confused expression. "Uh, sure, I guess. Tea sounds nice."

The woman claps her hands cheerfully. "Yay! Follow me!"

I let out a quiet sigh and slowly follow behind her. We walk through the hallway, and I notice a few other doors near the bedroom.

"Where do those doors lead?" I point at each one.

The woman stops in her tracks. "You'll know *soon enough*, but first...TEA!"

I'm not sure if I want to know soon enough.

The woman starts walking again, and from what I can see, her home is stunning! It's a two-level home with a door that I think leads to a basement. We turn the corner, and there's a small living room with an average sized kitchen next to it.

There are candles EVERYWHERE, so I'm guessing there's no power here, either. But since there are so many windows, there's a good amount of light in here.

"Your house is pretty."

She smiles. "Thank you. No one ever compliments it."

I slowly nod. It's not like I know what to say after a comment like that.

We make our way into the living room, and I hear a familiar tune playing nearby.

"Is that what I think it is…" I head in the direction of the sound, and there's a grand piano in the corner of the living room with a man playing one of Beethoven's symphonies.

"You play the piano well!"

The man looks over his shoulder and beams. I'm overtaken by his shiny, white teeth.

I can't believe his teeth are whiter than hers!

He stops playing the music and turns around, so that he's looking directly at me. "I see you enjoy classical music?" He nods his head with a gesture of approval and continues playing the piano.

I sit in a chair next to him. "Well, my best friend is into all of that. I just recognized the tune, because she'd listen to this type of music all the time!" I begin to recall Olivia lying on her bed listening to Beethoven. *Oh, what I would do to have those moments again.*

"Well, your best friend sounds like someone I'd like to be around!" he responds, without missing a beat on the piano. "By the way, my name is Johnathan. This is my wife, Rachel." He lifts one hand off the keys and points in her direction.

"Well, my name is—"

"Axel, we know. We saw your name engraved on your dog tag," Johnathan replies.

I immediately reach for my chain, but it's not around my neck! "Where's my dog tag?"

Rachel puts a hand on my shoulder. "Easy kid. It's with your clothes in the laundry room." She points up the stairs.

I go over to the stairs (which are directly across from the piano), and Johnathan steps in front of me.

"Look, Axel. We'll bring your clothes down soon. We just gave everything a nice wash and cleaned your dog tag in the sink. But you're not going to freely walk around our home. You are still a stranger."

I take a step back from the stairs. "Fine."

Johnathan smiles again. "Good. Everything's good. Now, would you like your tea?" He heads over to the island in the kitchen and hands me a mug filled with raspberry tea.

"Uh, thanks." I grab the cup and pretend to drink it. I have no idea who these people are, and I'm not going to drink or eat anything they give me (I've seen enough thrillers).

Johnathan clears his throat. "So, I'm guessing you're wondering how you ended up here with such wonderful hosts."

"Yeah, that's what I'm wondering..." I reply sarcastically.

Johnathan doesn't seem to notice. "Well, I was walking around in the snow when I noticed a fragile little boy curled up on the snowy ground." He reenacts the scene as if it was happening at this very moment.

Fragile, really?

He continues. "So, I carried you back to the cabin and brought two other boys in as well." He looks at the time on his watch, then opens the refrigerator.

I stare in disbelief. "You helped Weston and Jeremy too?"

Rachel smiles while taking a sip of her tea. "We try to help everyone we can."

Johnathan lets out a sigh and closes the refrigerator. "Yeah. The world has changed so much, but people should still try to help one another."

Rachel and Johnathan seem nice, but there's just something about them that doesn't sit well with me.

"Well, where are my friends?"

Johnathan puts an apron around his waist and grabs a can opener from off the counter. "They're somewhere around here, but first, let me prepare some food for you."

Rachel pulls two cans out of the pantry. "Would you like some chili?"

My stomach begins to growl. "Um, no thanks."

BOOM!

A loud noise erupts from under the ground. *Maybe it came from the basement?*

Johnathan and Rachel immediately make eye contact, and Rachel runs to the basement door and opens it.

"Excuse us for a moment." Johnathan brushes past me and follows Rachel downstairs.

Once the basement door closes, I ease off the chair and briefly look around. "I need to look for my weapons and supplies." I make my way over to the staircase.

I know Johnathan stopped me from coming up these stairs earlier, but I need my supplies and my clothes. I slowly lift one leg after the other, each step quieter than the next.

CREEK!

I stop in my tracks. *Was that me or the basement steps?* Either way, someone's gonna come up the stairs and notice me sneaking around. If these people ARE crazy, who knows what they'd do if they found out I was snooping, even if I was looking for my own belongings.

I dash down the stairs and race for the chair I was sitting in. As soon as I sit down, the basement door swings open. Johnathan walks over to me and places his hand calmly on my shoulder.

"Were you walking around up here?"

Oh great. I've always been terrible at lying. Probably because my mom drilled that lying was bad in my head since I was a little kid. But she did always say that if it was a life-or-death situation, it wasn't as bad. I think this is one of those situations.

I maintain eye contact with him. "I…was not…I w-was sitting here the whole t-time." I force a smile.

I know, I know. I completely blew it. I can imagine Olivia shaking her head in disapproval. *Only an idiot would believe the lie I just told.*

Johnathan's smile fades into a frown. "I don't like liars. Liars are untrustworthy." He cracks his knuckles.

Sweat pours down my forehead. "Okay, fine! I was going upstairs to grab my bookbag and my clothes. I was scared that you'd kick me out if you knew I was going upstairs." I maintain eye contact.

Johnathan's face turns back to the smile he once had, and he sits in the chair beside mine. "It is alright, Axel. I completely understand why a kid like you would panic over such things." He fixes his tie. "But I still will never tolerate liars. Go to your room, now." He points in the direction of *my room*, his smile fading once again.

I guess what he's saying is understandable, but all I was doing was getting my supplies. I shouldn't be punished for it.

I stand up from my chair with my back facing him. "I need my bookbag with ALL of my supplies in it," I demand.

311

I can hear Johnathan getting up from his chair. "Fine, I will bring it to you. Now go to your room," he states in an irritated tone.

Chapter 37:

Find a Way Out

I've been in this stupid room for hours now. I tried to open the door earlier, but they locked me in. Johnathan still hasn't given me my stuff either, and I haven't seen Jeremy or Weston yet. I just really need to find a way out of here and find them.

I pull on the door again in hopes of it being unlocked, but of course, it still isn't. I sit on the bed and try to think of a way out.

"Man, I know if Reese was here, he'd figure something out..." With all the drama, I totally forgot that Weston, Jeremy, and I were supposed to find Reese and make sure everything was alright with him. *Who knows where he is now?*

I grab a pillow and out of anger, I throw it at the wall.

CLANK!

"What was that?" I get up and ease closer to the pillow. "It must've hit something." I move the pillow out of the way, and there's a large vent on the bottom of the wall.

"How did I not see this before?"

I try to pull the vent cover off, but it's no use. There are screws on the vent cover, so it won't come off by pulling it. "There has to be some other way."

I bet there's no screwdrivers in here, but maybe there's something I can use in place of it. I open the closet door and still, there's nothing in here. I get on my hands and knees and rub my fingertips on the ground, hoping to find something on the carpet floor.

"Bingo!" I feel something under my fingertips and immediately reach for it. To my disappointment, I found two coins. "What am I supposed to do with this?" I vaguely remember seeing some guys on tv use coins instead of screwdrivers to unscrew something. *Maybe it will work for a vent, too?*

I use a coin and start unscrewing the screws from the vent, keeping my other hand on the vent to prevent it from falling. I finally unscrew the last screw, and the vent opens!

Looks like my luck is turning around! I carefully set the vent cover on the ground.

"Here goes nothing." I ease inside the vent, inching through the tight space. Thank goodness it's a larger vent, because if it wasn't, I would be stuck in that room for who knows how long.

I continue to crawl and notice another vent opening ahead of me. I ease closer and look through the gap. The kitchen and part of the living room are all that's visible. No trace of Johnathan or Rachel, so I highly doubt Jeremy and Wes are in here.

"I need to find the bedrooms." I back up and crawl in a different direction (I really need to stop talking to myself).

Soon enough, I see another vent cover in front of me, so I peak through the opening. To my surprise, Johnathan and Rachel are in a bedroom, talking in a quiet tone.

Rachel stares at herself in a mirror and starts applying makeup to her face. Her usual smile is now a sinister grin. "So, when are we going to feed that man to my aunt?" she asks nonchalantly.

"I don't know. We have to make sure it's either later on tonight or early tomorrow morning. We can't risk those idiotic kids hearing anything. Remember what happened when that Axel kid heard that loud noise? He used that to his advantage to snoop around! What would they do if they found out that we are feeding random survivors to our zombie relatives?"

Feeding? I immediately gag, but with all my might, I refrain from puking. I can't believe these psychos are feeding people to zombies! I need to get my friends out of here and save that man they're trying to feed to Rachel's zombie aunt!

I immediately start crawling in the opposite direction. *I need to find Jeremy and Weston!* I continue down the vent's path, and it leads me to two vent openings. I peak through the opening to my right and Weston's pacing back and forth in a bedroom that looks like the one I was in.

"Weston!" I whisper as I lightly bang on the vent.

Weston's eyes wander for a minute, but then he squints at the vent.

"Over here!" I mutter.

Weston bends down in front of the vent. "Axel! I thought you were dead!" he whispers cheerfully.

"Yeah, these creeps saved me, but they have—"

"An ulterior motive, I know. Figured it out the moment I woke up."

"Good for you, but can you use these coins to unscrew the vent? It's getting kinda crammed in here." I push the coins through the gap in the vent.

Weston grabs the coins and starts unscrewing the vent fast and efficiently. He pulls the vent opening off and tosses it to the side.

I crawl out of the vent and stretch my arms and legs. "Thanks. Gosh, it was tight in there."

Weston stares at me with anticipation. "So, what did you find out? Don't leave me in the dark!"

"They're feeding people to zombies!"

Weston instantly holds his fist over his mouth. "That's disgusting...I think I'm gonna puke."

"Save it for when we leave. Jeremy's here too, and we need to find—"

"Jeremy's here? Well, what are we waiting for?" Weston cracks his knuckles.

"I think his room is nearby, so we need to be fast but quiet. The two psychos are still awake." I crawl back into the vent and peak through the other ventilation opening.

Just as I suspected, Jeremy is in a room that looks identical to ours. He's fast asleep on the bed, snoring and all.

"Is he seriously sleeping?! Wake up Jeremy!" Weston bangs on the vent aggressively.

"Sh, Wes!"

All I can do is hope that they didn't hear anything.

Jeremy's eyes open and he rubs them. "What's all the commotion..."

"Are you really that delusional?" Weston whispers, but loud enough for Jeremy to hear.

Jeremy immediately grabs his glasses, then crawls over to the vent. He then grabs a coin from his pocket and unscrews the vent.

I scratch my head in confusion. "How did you know how to do that?"

"Come on Axel, it's common knowledge. I learned how to do this when I was three!"

"And yet you didn't know how to use a gun when this whole apocalyptic mess started." Weston rolls his eyes. "Can you hurry up?"

"Technically, I knew how to use a gun, I just never used one personally." Jeremy pushes the vent opening to the side, and we crawl out.

"What's going on, guys? I'm really confused." Jeremy sits on the bed.

Weston turns the knob on the bedroom door, but it's locked. "All you need to know is that these people are insane, and we need to go."

Jeremy taps his finger on his chin. "But these people seem nice, are you sure they're crazy? We could have died if it wasn't for them!"

"Sorry to tell you, but they are nothing but crazy. They're feeding people to zombies," I tell him.

Jeremy covers his mouth with his hands. "That's just... gross."

Weston stands beside the vent. "Tell me about it. Now less talking, more finding our bags and getting the heck out of here." He crawls back through the vent.

319

"Where is he going? We need to stay together!" Jeremy quickly follows behind him.

"Well, looks like we're going now." I crawl through the vent and follow closely behind Jeremy.

Chapter 38:

<u>Who's in the Basement?</u>

"Bingo."

Weston stops in front of the vent opening that leads to the kitchen. He lifts his leg up and starts kicking the vent door.

"What are you doing? They'll hear that!" I whisper frantically.

"How else are we supposed to get out?" He continues kicking the vent until the door flies off and slides across the hardwood floor.

"They might not have heard the banging, but they definitely heard that," Jeremy gulps.

Weston crawls out of the vent and looks around the house. "Too nice of a house to have crazy people living in it." He tiptoes up the stairs and down a hallway.

"Weston! We're supposed to stay together, remember?" I frown, quietly following behind him with Jeremy right behind me.

I quietly go up the stairs and notice two doors across from each other. Weston looks at both doors and opens one of them.

"Dude! You can't just open random doors like that!" Jeremy whispers.

"Well, maybe I just had a hunch that our supplies would be in here." Weston pushes the door fully open, and our bookbags are lying on the floor!

I reach for my bookbag and search through it. "Thank you, God. Everything's in here. What about you guys?" I put my dog tag necklace back on.

"All my stuff is here. What about you Weston?" Jeremy puts his bag on his shoulders.

"Yup. Everything's here. Let's leave this dump," Weston leaves the room and heads down the stairs. Jeremy follows him, and they both reach the foot of the stairs.

"Guys, wait!" I reach my hand out.

Weston stops in his tracks. "What is it? Can it wait?"

"Well, I heard the psychos talking, and they're going to feed some guy to the zombies!"

Weston doesn't seem bothered. "Sounds like a personal problem. We gotta go, man!" He reaches for the front door handle.

Jeremy looks back at me. "Yeah, I'm inclined to agree with Weston! That's just too risky, Axel!"

"But we can't just leave him in the basement to die!" I rush over to the basement door.

"Fine Axel. But if I die, it's your fault!" Jeremy squirms.

I'll make sure nothing happens to you Jeremy. It's the least I can do.

Weston opens the front door. "I'm sorry guys, but that's just a risk I'm not willing to take. I have a little sister to look out for! You mentioned you have a little brother Axel. You shouldn't take risks like this either. He needs you."

I open the basement door and stare down the steps. *August does need me.* He needs his older brother, but it just doesn't sit well with my conscience to leave that man down there.

323

"I agree with you Wes, but I have to do this." I go down the basement stairs, not waiting for a rebuttal.

"This is really eerie," Jeremy mumbles as he tiptoes down the stairs.

"Tell me about it." I reach the bottom of the stairs and see a man tied up.

He has a gag around his mouth, preventing him from speaking. The more my eyes adjust to the darkness, the more I can see the man, and to my surprise, it's Reese!

"Reese! What the heck are you doing tied up?!" I run to him, but he frantically shakes his head. "Reese, why are you…"

"WATCH OUT!" Jeremy pulls me back just as a zombie's hand reaches out and tries to grab me!

"Whoa!" I back up and when I look closer, I see multiple zombies chained to a wall on the opposite side. I look back at Reese. His hands are tied to a rope that's hanging from the ceiling.

"If you ease your way towards Reese, maybe you'll be able to avoid the zombies?" Jeremy wonders.

"That's a risky move. Maybe I should just move along the wall on this side. That way the zombies can't reach me," I explain.

"Sound like a better plan than mine!"

I put my back up against the wall on this side, so that I'm across from the zombies, and I ease toward Reese. This kinda reminds me of an action movie. The main character scaling across the side of a skyscraper, avoiding gunfire. Except, I'm not ten stories up, I'm in a basement. And I'm not avoiding bullets; I'm avoiding zombie hands from pulling me straight to my doom.

The zombies try to grab me, but to no avail! I make it across and take the duct tape from around Reese' mouth off. Without his bandana around his mouth, he looks less like a bandit and more like a regular civilian.

Reese looks past me. "Behind you..."

I turn around and Johnathan and Rachel are near the basement stairs, staring at us. Jeremy quivers with fear and eases his way over to me.

"Why did you kids have to go snooping in places you shouldn't? Everything could have been fine." Johnathan twirls a knife around in his hand.

325

These people don't scare me. With all my courage, I remain calm. "Why are you feeding people to zombies?" I counter.

Rachel chuckles at my question. "We aren't just feeding people to these zombies for no reason. These are our relatives. They need to eat to survive, so we feed them random survivors, like that man beside you, so they can live." She makes it seem so practical and completely fine to do something like this.

"You both are insane! These are monsters! They are no longer your relatives!" Jeremy blurts out. "You don't even know if zombies need to eat to survive!"

While Jeremy has them distracted, I grab a knife from out of my bookbag and start cutting the rope that's tying Reese up, and he falls to the ground.

"You morons! The zombies will be angry! You will pay for this!" Johnathan charges right for us and aims his knife at Jeremy!

No, this won't happen again. *I let Jeffrey down, but I won't do the same to Jeremy!*

I push Jeremy out of the way, and Reese snatches his gun from his holster and shoots Johnathan!

POW!

Johnathan holds his stomach and falls to the ground, unresponsive.

Reese lowers his gun. "I guess they forgot to...remove my gun from my holster." He breathes heavily.

"YOU KILLED HIM!" Rachel pulls her gun out of her pocket and aims it right at Reese!

"No!" I shout.

Out of nowhere, Weston charges down the stairs and pushes Rachel into the arms of the zombies.

"AHHHH!" The zombies pull Rachel closer to them and start biting her.

Jeremy covers his mouth. "This is a very unpleasant sight. Can we please go?"

"Yeah, let's go guys..." Reese slowly gets off the ground and heads upstairs.

. . . .

We found some more supplies and a map in the house that showed the exact location of where we were. I was grateful, because we were no longer lost, and since I know the coordinates of the cabin, we would be able to head there with no problems.

"Reese? Are you alright? You seem tired and weak." I look at him with concern.

He places his bandana back around his face. "Yeah, I'm fine. They just beat me up a little, but I'll be alright. At least I'm not zombie food."

I scratch the back of my head. "Why do you keep that bandana on?"

Reese shrugs his shoulders as we continue walking. "No particular reason, I just like it. It always intimidates bad people, so that's a plus," he winks.

"Yeah, but how are we supposed to find the gas station? We were unconscious when they took us to their house."

Reese scratches his arm. "I was super weak because of the cold, but I wasn't unconscious. Our mysterious "saviors" helped me to their home, and it's not far from the gas station at all. Just keep following me."

"Then it all works out, then." I smile and slow down my pace, so it meets with Weston's. "Thanks for coming back."

Weston nods his head. "Don't mention it, Axel. But to be honest, you guys would be *dead* if I didn't go down there." His smile fades. "This hurts my pride to say this, but I shouldn't have let you guys go down there by yourselves in the first place."

I stop in my tracks. "Hey, don't worry about it. What matters is that you came when you did."

"I guess, but we're a team, and we should stay together. Plus, I'm glad you guys didn't listen to me. Reese would've died if you did."

I agree. "Yeah, I knew something just felt off about not going in that basement."

Jeremy comes from behind and puts his arms around both me and Weston. "I'm just glad we're done with all of this, so we can finally go to that cabin you and Olivia have been talking about!"

I smile. "Yeah, I can't wait to see my family!"

Jeremy grins. "I can't wait to meet them!"

Chapter 39:

<u>Arrival</u>

It's only been a day since we left the gas station. We've been traveling at a fast pace, so we've been making good time! I'm just so excited to finally reach the cabin!

"The cabin should be visible any minute now," I tell them while leading the group.

Olivia's walking right beside me, practically jumping up and down since we're almost there. "You did it Axel," she exclaims.

I wrinkle my forehead. "Did what? Remembered where the cabin was?"

"Well, yes, but you promised our parents that you'd look out for me and that we'd stay together, and we did! Thanks, Axe." She puts her arm around mine.

"I always keep my promises!"

Weston puts one arm around his little sister, and the other arm around Jeremy. "Just so you guys know, I look at all of you as family now."

"Same here. I look out for you guys like my own," Reese grins.

"There it is!" Olivia rushes to the cabin.

"The cabin!" I take off running and racing after Olivia.

"Why are we standing here? Let's race there, too!!" Willow shouts.

The rest of the group run behind us, stomping on the snowy ground.

I can't believe it…Mom, Hayden, and August are right in there. This long journey from Georgia was worth it. Man, I've missed them so much.

Olivia swings the door open. "Mom, Dad? Are you here?" She walks around the cabin and notices boxes of food and a letter on the table.

I notice the silence that follows Olivia's comment. "Mom? Hayden? We're here!"

Olivia's voice lowers. "Where are they?"

I shrug. "They have to be around here somewhere."

She nods her head and continues walking around, checking to see if they're in here. I pick up a letter that's on the table.

"Axel, if you're reading this, I love you so much! I hope you have conquered this world's plague. I knew I shouldn't have let you go to Georgia...But I guess it's too late now. I hope you and Olivia are still together, and I hope you guys are praying constantly, because you know we need God to guide us through this. When you both left, I was so nervous. I felt very uneasy letting you go so far away from me, but Hayden reassured me, and August made every day go by easier.

"I couldn't shake the feeling that was inside of me ab-out the "conspiracy theory," but Justine kept telling me that I was just paranoid. A couple of days passed, and this "zom-bie apocalypse" was all over the news! It was affecting so many states on the East Coast, and we knew we had to get to you guys quickly! But the government stopped all flights, so I knew I had to drive to get to you. But then you called me, and asked me not to head to Georgia, that you'd be fine...So I didn't, which I still feel was the wrong thing to do.

"We began to pack our things, and we were on our way to the cabin like you said! Olivia's parents, Justine and Kyle, hitched a ride with us. There was no point in using multiple cars for one destination. The journey was tough! Hayden and Kyle looked out for us so much, and August was always whi-ning, but what can you expect from a four-year-old? Anyway, a few days ago it started to hail, then the snow started falling. At times I was giving up hope, but Hayden kept telling me that you guys would be here soon. I hope we reunite again my baby boy…I miss you so much, and I know you feel the same. I wrote this letter in case you come when I'm looking for supplies."

Trust in God.

-Mom.

"Ps. August ran off somewhere! I'll be back soon. Don't come looking for me, just stay at the cabin!"

I look at the letter and sigh. "I hope you guys found August and are heading back now…" I look over and see Reese standing by the doorway.

"Your mom's letter?" He points to the paper in my hand.

"Yeah, she isn't here. My little brother ran off, so they all went after him. Hopefully they find him safe and sound."

Reese glances at the letter. "Hopefully."

"I'm sure they're alright," Weston reassures.

Olivia walks out of a bedroom and hands me another letter. "My parents wrote me a letter also."

I quickly read it and realize it has similar information to my mom's letter.

Olivia takes her pink hat off and sets it on the table. "I guess we should just stay here until they get back, since that's what they said. Even though I really want to go looking for them."

Weston slouches on the couch. "I'm sure they're fine. They've survived this long."

Willow nods in agreement. "Yeah, your little brother couldn't have gone far, don't worry!"

I smile at all of them.

"So, this was the cabin you guys have been talking about the whole time?" Jeremy admires all the antique furniture.

"Yeah, I'm glad you guys get to see it." I take a seat beside Weston on the couch.

"So, what's our plan once the family comes back?" Weston folds his arms.

"Well, I haven't really thought the rest through…" I sigh.

"We'll cross that bridge once we get to it. For now, let's just take a moment to relax." Reese lays on the mat in the middle of the floor.

"So, after all this time, I don't think we know much about each other. We've got nothing but time, so let's share some stuff," Weston chuckles. "I told Axel a little about my past. Me and Willow were raised by our mom, that's basically the only interesting part."

"Yup, pretty much," Willow leans her head on Weston.

Weston looks at Olivia. "What about you? I'm surprised you've kept your personal life to yourself all this time."

Olivia shrugs her shoulders and rubs her fingernails. "Eh, there's not much to talk about. My parents are two very successful businesspeople, and they raised a very successful daughter," she points at herself. "I've known Axel almost my whole life, which I'm sure I've mentioned before, and I ran track. That's basically it."

Jeremy smiles. "Sounds like a good life."

"I guess," Olivia replies dryly.

Weston faces me. "Well, what's your story?"

"My story?" I never really wanted to mention much about my past. It's not like it's a happy story like Olivia's. I prefer keeping it to myself, but he's right. We should know a little more about each other.

"Well, I was raised by my mom. My parents got a divorce before I was born, and my dad never knew about me."

"Why didn't your mom just tell him about you?" Weston asks.

"Heh, that's a long, complicated story. Basically, my parents lost contact. It was a tough divorce for them both, so they stopped talking. Once my mom found out about me, she couldn't reach him."

Jeremy listens in disbelief. "Sounds confusing."

Olivia nods her head in agreement. "Tell me about it. I've known him for years, and the story is still complicated."

I chuckle at their responses. "Yeah, that's why I gave you guys the short version."

Weston raises his hand. "Wait, but you mentioned a little brother a few weeks ago. How does he tie in?"

"He's my mom and stepdad's kid."

"Oh," Weston doesn't press any further on the topic. "Alright, what about you, Reese? Got any kids of your own?"

Reese sits up. "I always wanted a kid, but no, I don't."

Willow raises an eyebrow. "Married?"

"Divorced, and Axel, I can relate to your parents. After some divorces, you just can't bear to communicate anymore."

I nod. "Makes sense."

"Any family?" Jeremy wonders.

"I'm not that close with them. I haven't visited them in years."

I think of a question myself. "If you did have a kid, would you want a boy or a girl?"

Reese thinks for a little bit. "A boy for sure. I could teach him all sorts of things that a daughter wouldn't get."

I nod intently. "Yeah, you'd make a good dad, Reese."

Reese's face beams. "You think so? Thanks."

Jeremy sighs deeply as he listens. He seems deep in thought.

I look at Jeremy. "You alright, bud?"

"Not really, I wish Jeffrey didn't wander off. I was hoping he'd be here like he said, but he's not...I hope nothing happened to him." He takes his glasses off and rubs his eyes.

When he doesn't have his glasses on, he looks identical to Jeffrey (not that they don't already look alike).

I hold back tears. "Jeremy... I have to tell you something..."

"How about we all get some rest? We've been walking for hours and should probably get some sleep," Reese gives me a disapproving look.

"He's right! There are two bedrooms with two beds in each, so good luck fighting for those!" Olivia shouts as she races up the stairs, Jeremy right behind her.

Reese looks at me with concern. "You shouldn't tell him, at least not yet. The kid's not strong enough to handle something like that. Most people aren't," he whispers.

338

"I guess you're right."

"Yup. On a better note, I'll stay up in case your family comes back." Reese pats my back and leans his head on the mat.

Weston stands up and stretches his arms. "Ready to head upstairs?"

"Never been more ready."

This whole experience has been a rollercoaster. Sometimes I felt good about everything, thinking that things were going to go back to normal, and other times I felt sick to my stomach, knowing that things were never going to go back. Even if that's the case, my *'framily'* has helped me get through this. Whether it was saving my life or being my moral support. Either way, I've needed both and gotten both. If it weren't for them, I wouldn't be here.

I open one of the bedroom doors, and Willow and Olivia are sharing a bed.

"Come on, Axe! Sleep in here!" Olivia throws a pillow at me and so does Willow.

I turn around and look at Weston. "I know your little sister's in here. Do you want to sleep in here with her?"

Weston laughs. "Nah, I need a break from her anyway, and I know you guys will look out for her."

Willow throws a pillow at Weston. "You're so dumb!"

He laughs and goes inside the other bedroom.

I lay my head down on the other bed. Maybe I'll finally get some good rest, because I haven't gotten any in a long time.

"Goodnight, Axel!" Olivia and Willow tell me as they close their eyes.

I smile. "Night girls! Goodnight Jeremy, Reese, and Weston!"

"Hush! I'm trying to sleep here!" Weston yells from the other room.

"Such a cranky pants! Goodnight Axel and everyone else!" Jeremy exclaims from the other room.

"More like good afternoon!" Reese shouts from downstairs.

I smile at all their responses. Things didn't turn out the way I thought, but I least I have great people to stand alongside me. I slowly close my eyes, in hopes that this adventure will have a happy ending.

Thank you!

I want to thank all of you who read the whole book! I put my heart and soul into it, and I hope you enjoyed it as much as I loved writing it! I want to thank my parents for reminding me to never give up on my dreams, and that no dream is ever too big! I want to thank my siblings for inspiring me and encouraging me to complete this book, and I also want to thank my friends who supported me when I told them about my book! I can't wait to show you more of my work to come, and once again, thank you for reading this book!

About the author:

Aléce Land is an author under the publishing company, Jai Publishing LLC. She debuted her first novel, *Humanity's End* soon after her eighteenth birthday. She is currently working on her next novel and will soon be starting her third year of college.